ook i
we
ho

zpe

2 7

I ₋ M

+к·x

1

Sebastiano drew her even closer, releasing the lapels of his jacket to slide his hands into the wisps of hair either side of her face. She stopped laughing instantly, her eyes suddenly wide as saucers. Her hair felt like silk against his fingers, her skin even softer. His eyes drifted from her mouth to the tiny pulse-point flickering at the base of her throat, a sense of victory he couldn't explain coursing through him.

'Kind of funny, you think?'

'Sebastiano…?' Her voice was soft and her hands came up to grip his thick wrists. 'What are you doing?'

'I'm going to give you a lesson in what I would do if this relationship was real.'

Only it's one hundred per cent fake, he reminded himself—right before he bent to her and covered her mouth with his.

Her petal-soft lips parted on a gasp of surprise, her body stiffening beneath the onslaught. Sebastiano gathered her closer, feeling her rigidity give way to a trembling need as old as time.

He groaned, pressing his lips harder over hers, seeking access to the warm recesses of her mouth. 'Open for me, Poppy,' he growled. 'Kiss me as I've imagined you doing this past week. Let me taste you, *bella*. Let me—'

Another groan escaped his lips as she did as he requested, willingly parting her mouth for him, a tiny whimper escaping her lips as his tongue swept inside.

With two university degrees and a variety of false career starts under her belt, **Michelle Conder** decided to satisfy her lifelong desire to write and finally found her dream job. She currently lives in Melbourne, Australia, with one super-indulgent husband, three self-indulgent but exquisite children, a menagerie of over-indulged pets, and the intention of doing some form of exercise daily. She loves to hear from her readers at michelleconder.com.

Books by Michelle Conder

Mills & Boon Modern Romance

Defying the Billionaire's Command
Hidden in the Sheikh's Harem
The Most Expensive Lie of All
Duty at What Cost?
Living the Charade
His Last Chance at Redemption

One Night With Consequences

Prince Nadir's Secret Heir

Scandal in the Spotlight

Girl Behind the Scandalous Reputation

Visit the Author Profile page
at millsandboon.co.uk for more titles.

THE
ITALIAN'S VIRGIN
ACQUISITION

BY
MICHELLE CONDER

First Published in Great Britain 2017
By Mills & Boon, an imprint of HarperCollins*Publishers*
1 London Bridge Street, London, SE1 9GF

© 2017 Michelle Conder

ISBN: 978-0-263-06970-9

Printed and bound in Great Britain
by CPI Antony Rowe, Chippenham, Wiltshire

THE
ITALIAN'S VIRGIN
ACQUISITION

Thank you to Laura, my beautiful editor,
who deserves amazing things to happen in her life.

CHAPTER ONE

SEBASTIANO CHECKED HIS Rolex as he strode into SJC Towers, his London office building, completely oblivious to the wintry rain landing like icy pellets on his face. From the moment he'd woken up he'd known it was going to be an interesting day. Interesting as in the Chinese curse 'interesting'—not 'it's going to be great' interesting. Not that he held much with curses or proverbs.

But he wasn't going to let noisy workmen, an unexpected early-morning visit from his now ex-mistress or a flat tyre derail him. He had been waiting for over two years for this day and finally his crusty old grandfather was going to give up on his stubbornness and hand over the reins of the family dynasty. And not before time!

Bert, his weekend security chief, gave him a nod as he approached the reception desk, not at all perplexed to see his boss arriving for work on a Sunday morning.

'Catch the game yesterday, boss?' Bert asked with a flashing grin.

'Don't gloat,' Sebastiano advised. 'It's a very unattractive quality.'

Bert's grin widened. 'Yes sir!'

Their friendly rivalry was a source of great amusement to Sebastiano. Too often those around him hid behind a mask of eager deference to get on his good side all because he had been born into a life of wealth and privilege. It was irritating to say the least.

He caught a glimpse of the newspaper Bert had spread out on the desk showing a picture of Sebastiano leaving a posh, and utterly boring, cocktail party the night before. Evidently his now ex-mistress had seen the same photos on the Internet which was why she had decided to ambush him outside his Park Lane home after his early-morning run, wanting to know why he hadn't invited her to attend with him.

In hindsight, *'because it didn't occur to me'* hadn't been his best answer. Things had rapidly deteriorated after that, ending when she'd issued him with an ultimatum: either move their relationship forward or end it. Not that he could blame her for being frustrated. He'd pursued her a month ago with the ruthless determination that had seen him rise to the top of the *Forbes 500* list by the age of thirty-one and he'd yet to sleep with her more than once.

Which wasn't like him. He normally had a very healthy libido but he'd been off stride lately. Probably only this damned situation with his grandfather. Not to mention the twenty-hour days he had been putting in at the office to finalise a deal that would see him take over as industry leader in the hotel construction market.

Of course, he'd apologised to the world-renowned ballerina, but she hadn't been impressed, blowing him a kiss over one elegant shoulder and purring that it was his loss as she had gracefully exited his life. Thinking about it now, he might suggest she give break-up lessons to some of his past involvements. She'd make a small fortune teaching basic relationship-exiting etiquette to others, particularly to the Spanish model who had thrown her hair brush at him when he'd suggested they part ways some months back.

'Better luck next time, eh, boss?' Bert chortled, feigning contrition. Sebastiano grunted. He knew Bert was referring to yesterday's football match, in which his team had annihilated Sebastiano's, but equally he could have applied the sentiment to his stalled sex life.

'Your team wins again,' Sebastiano said as he headed for the bank of elevators. 'I'll dock your wages by half.'

'Yes sir!' Bert's grin widened as he checked the security monitors on his desk.

Stepping into the lift, Sebastiano stabbed the button for his floor and hoped that his adroit EA had found time to collate the reports he wanted to present to his grandfather this morning as part of his winning pitch. Ordinarily he'd never ask Paula to come in on a Sunday, but his grandfather had landed this visit on him at the last minute and he hadn't wanted to leave anything to chance.

Not that his business acumen was the reason behind his grandfather's reticence to hand him control of the company. No, what he wanted was to see Sebastiano settled down with a lovely *donna* who would one day become the mother of his multiple *bambini*. His grandfather wanted him to have something other than work to sustain him. Something called work-life balance. A modern-day catch cry if ever Sebastiano had heard one, and one he suspected his grandfather had acquired from his cherished wife. Whatever Nonna wanted, Nonna got.

'How can I expect you to take on another demanding role when you already have so little time to relax?' his grandfather had said over the phone a month ago. 'Your grandmother and I just want to see you happy, Bastian. You know how we worry. I can't die if I don't know you will be taken care of.'

'You know I can take care of myself,' Sebastiano had growled. 'And you're not dying. At least, not right now.'

But his grandparents were old-world Italian. If there wasn't a good woman cooking in his kitchen and warming his bed at night, they considered him to be living a lonely, substandard existence. And apparently having a housekeeper providing those hot meals, and as many women as a man could want offering to warm his bed, wasn't what they were talking about.

More's the pity.

Because for Sebastiano being busy *was* his work-life balance. He thrived on it. There wasn't a day went by he didn't wake up wanting to conquer some new business opportunity or some new corporate challenge. Love? Marriage? Both required a level of intimacy he didn't have it in him to give.

Being a little removed from those around him had served him well over the years and he couldn't see a reason to change that. And if some nights he had a lonely, late-night aperitif by himself, overlooking the glittering lights of whichever city he happened to be in at the time... well, so be it.

Right now he was in the prime of his life, and as he had just bought Britain's largest steel and concrete supply company there was no better time to take over as head of Castiglione Europa. The two businesses dovetailed so beautifully that Sebastiano had already asked his marketing and sales team to work up a plan to move into the hotel refurbishment industry across Eastern Europe.

He just had to convince his hard-headed *nonno* to retire and see out his twilight years with the wife he adored in the family's Amalfi coast villa. Then, and only then, could Sebastiano make up for the hardship he had caused his family fifteen years ago.

Deep in thought, he flicked on the lights to the executive floor and heard a text come through on his phone. Switching on the coffee machine on his way to his office, he opened the text and pulled up short.

He read it twice. Apparently Paula was in Accident and Emergency with her husband who had a suspected broken ankle. The report he required was still on her computer.

His frown turned into a scowl. With his grandfather due any minute, he didn't need this kind of delay.

Texting back that he hoped her husband was okay, he retrieved her laptop from her desk and carried it into his office. Glancing at the screen festooned with multi-coloured icons that made his eyes cross, he couldn't find any folder that looked like it held the report he needed.

Great. That was just great.

Poppy checked the Mickey Mouse watch on her wrist and groaned. She had to get out of here. Her brother Simon would be waiting and he always became agitated when she was late. On top of that Maryann, her wonderful neighbour who had been more of a mother to both of them than anyone else they had ever known, had just been diagnosed with MS. It was a cruel blow for a woman who was beautiful both inside and out and Poppy wanted to do something nice for her today.

Trying not to dwell on the awful news, Poppy tightened her haphazard ponytail and skimmed over the legal brief she wanted to present to her boss tomorrow morning. She only had one week left of her internship at SJC International and she wanted to make sure she sparkled. Who knew, once her law degree was finished she might even be offered a job here if she impressed the powers that be enough. The ultimate power being her boss's boss, Sebastiano Castiglione. She hadn't had anything to do with him directly, but she had seen him stalking through the halls, his long stride indicating a man who was always on a mission, his wide shoulders denoting that likely he would succeed at that mission.

Catching herself daydreaming about his dark bad-boy good looks, and reminding herself that he had a bad-boy reputation to match, she stacked the files she had been using back in the cabinet and switched off the computer.

Not being a morning person, she would have liked to work from home this morning, but the laptop she used for university was a thousand years old and wouldn't run the program she needed to use. On top of which intern privileges didn't extend to downloading company files on her private device, even if she was doing company business.

Stretching the kinks out of her neck, she was about to leave when she noticed the legal book she had borrowed from Paula a week earlier. Tomorrow was going to be a hectic day so it made sense to return it on her way out today.

Ordinarily she wouldn't have access to the big boss's hallowed ground, but since her boss had lent her his access pass she did. Still, she hesitated for a second. She didn't want to get Mr Adams into trouble by doing something she shouldn't, but she also didn't want to risk the chance she would return the book late and look sloppy. One of the best ways to stand out as an intern was to be as efficient as possible and Poppy took her job very seriously. And, since no one else was around this morning, who would know?

Making her mind up, she grabbed the book and headed for the lift. After having been raised in the foster care system since she was twelve, and having to take care of a brother ten years younger who had been born deaf, she knew the only way out of her current poverty-riddled existence was to focus on bettering herself. She'd been given a second chance when Maryann had found them both huddled up to a heater at Paddington Station eight years ago and she intended to use every second of that chance to make sure that they both had a future to look forward to.

Swiping the access card and pressing the button for the executive floor, she waited patiently for the lift to open out onto the stylish elegance that denoted that one had truly arrived in the world. Crossing the softly carpeted floor into Mr Castiglione's outer office, Poppy paused to take in the sweeping views of London she so rarely got to see. Despite the pale grey sky the city looked picture-perfect with its seamless blend of new-and old-world architecture. It was as if nothing could touch a person from way up here, but Poppy knew that, once you got down to ground level, things could not only touch you; they could destroy you if you let them.

Caught up as she was by dark, unwanted memories, she jumped when a deep male voice cursed loudly, shattering the stillness.

Heart thumping, Poppy turned to find who it was, but no one was about. Then another curse coloured the air and she realised it was coming from inside her boss's office.

Always too curious for her own good, she stepped forward on light feet and paused at the open doorway to Mr Castiglione's internal space. She sucked in a sharp breath as she saw the man himself standing, legs braced wide, in front of the plate glass windows.

She'd recognise him anywhere, of course. Powerful. Untamed. Stunningly good-looking. He raked a hand through his hair, mussing it into untidy black waves. He was tall for an Italian, and muscular, as if he worked out every day and then some. Since he was reputed to work about twenty hours a day, Poppy didn't know where he found the time, but she was glad he did. He was eye-candy extraordinaire. Or 'sex on a stick', as Maryann was wont to say.

As if he sensed her silent perusal, he shot round from studying the phone in his hand, his brilliant green eyes piercing her straight to her core. For a moment Poppy forgot to breathe. Then he spoke, his aggravated gaze sweeping over her and lighting tiny spot fires of sensation in its wake.

'Who the hell are you?'

'I'm an intern.' Poppy cleared the frog from her throat. 'Poppy. Poppy Connolly. I work for you.'

His frown deepened as he looked her up and down again.

'Since when have jeans and a sweater been considered appropriate office attire?'

Poppy flushed at the dressing down. 'It's a Sunday,' she explained, forcing herself not to tuck thick strands of her untidy brown hair behind her ear. 'And I wasn't expecting anyone else to be in.' Which wasn't really much of an explanation when he stood before her in a snowy-white dress shirt, red tie and dark trousers that did little to hide his powerful thighs.

'Yes, it is a Sunday. So why are you here?'

'I have a week left and I wanted to finish up a presentation for Mr Adams. He said it would be fine if I came in.'

One dark eyebrow rose. 'Taking dedication a bit far, isn't it?'

'Not if you want to get ahead,' she said simply. 'And I'd love to work here when I graduate. Being flexible and committed are just two of the things interns can do to stand out.'

Sure that he was about to toss her out of his office, maybe via one of those plate glass windows, she was surprised when instead he asked, 'What are the others?'

'Be punctual, treat the position like a job and dress for success.' She ticked off each item on her fingers.

His gaze fell to her ancient skinny jeans and Poppy tried not to cringe. When she had first started at SJC five weeks ago she had imagined one day meeting this man, who was reported to be some sort of corporate god, but in her imaginings it hadn't quite gone like this.

'Broke that one, I see,' he said sardonically.

Poppy felt heat creep into her cheeks and realised that her heart was beating at double its normal rate. Probably 'finding your boss attractive' wasn't on that special intern's list either, and she tried to crank up the wheels of her sluggish brain to think of a way to salvage the rapidly deteriorating situation.

When the phone rang on his desk it broke the taught

silence between them and also threw Poppy a welcome lifeline.

'Let me get that,' she said in her most businesslike manner.

Before he could respond, she had made it to his desk and snatched up the phone. She smiled widely at him as she chirped, 'Mr Castiglione's office,' in her most professional voice.

Her smile dimmed as she strained to listen to the teary sound of a woman on the other end of the line. She had a heavily accented voice and, coupled with her distress, Poppy could just make out, 'Sorry to interrupt,' and, 'Is Sebastiano in?'

'Yes, he is here,' Poppy said, all too aware that the man they were discussing had not taken his eyes off her. 'Yes, of course. Just a moment.' Not knowing which button on the handset was the mute, she held out the phone. 'It's for you,' she half-whispered.

Once more his eyebrow climbed his forehead. 'What a surprise.'

Feeling as if she had mucked up again, she stepped back from his radiating warmth as he moved closer and took the phone.

'Yes?' he barked into it.

Seeing his scowl instantly deepen, Poppy decided to take the initiative and make him a coffee. She had noticed the red light glowing on the coffee machine in his outer office and, since there was no cup on his desk, it stood to reason that he'd intended to make one but hadn't had the time.

Well, she would fix that and earn herself some Brownie points in the process. Maybe some of the ones she had lost handing him a call that, now that she thought about, was most likely from his current girlfriend. Or ex, given that the woman was crying. His short-term conquests were the stuff of legend around the office. As was the expensive break-up-and-move-on jewellery he supposedly got Paula to buy for them at the end.

Eager to get home and check on Simon, and give Maryann a hug and a cup of tea, she hurried to the coffee machine, surprised to find her boss still on the call when she set the cup down beside him. He passed a weary hand through his hair and she was inordinately pleased with herself for thinking of the coffee when he suddenly reached out and manacled her wrist with his large hand, preventing her from leaving.

Poppy instantly stilled, staring down at his darkly tanned fingers that were now idly stroking the soft skin on the inside of her wrist. Her breath hitched as darts of wicked pleasure shot up her arm. Her eyes shot to his and she could tell by the way his brilliant green eyes narrowed that he had registered her heated reaction.

Lust turned her knees to water. Lust and disbelief because, not only was this man her current boss, but he was listening to a woman—who she was now pretty certain was his girlfriend—sobbing on the end of the phone while caressing her!

Louse!

Annoyed that she had felt such pleasure given the circumstances, Poppy jerked her hand back, knocking over the coffee mug she had only moments ago set so carefully in front of him. Before either of them could react, the contents of the mug went flying over the desk, dark liquid splattering all over the front of her boss's pristine white shirt.

Sebastiano let out an explosive round of Italian curse words that made Poppy blush even though she didn't understand a single one of them.

She stared open-mouthed as he hung up his call, holding his sopping wet shirt away from his chest.

'What the hell was that?' he ground out, fury splitting the air between them.

'I… You…' Glancing around wildly, Poppy grabbed a wad of tissues from a side cabinet and started dabbing at his chest. When he held his hand up for her to stop, she noticed that drops had splashed down onto his crotch and, without thinking, she dabbed at the offending liquid only to have that hand manacle her wrist again. This time without the light stroking.

'There's a shirt hanging in the closet behind you. Get it.'

Glancing up into his irritated gaze, Poppy felt a fresh wave of heat fill her cheeks. The air seemed to thicken and crackle between them like heat shimmering off concrete on a hot day. 'Yes, sorry. I…'

'Any time today would be good,' he growled.

'Right,' she stammered.

Even more annoyed with herself, she reached into his closet and ripped the clear plastic from a fresh shirt, not at all ready to turn around and find her boss shirtless and wiping his ripped, tanned abdomen with another wad of tissues.

Good God, the man had sheets of muscles layered on top of more muscles, and all of that bronzed, fit perfection was covered in a pelt of healthy dark hair that arrowed down…

'I— You—' She pointed to the vicinity of his torso. 'You have a red mark on your chest. Do you want me to get some salve for it?'

'No, I do not want you to do anything else,' he bit out.

'Okay.' Poppy thrust the shirt at him, turning her burning face away, hoping he couldn't hear her thundering heartbeat. 'I—I'm sorry,' she stammered, her throat tight with embarrassment. 'I don't know what happened. I'm not usually so clumsy—really I'm not—but when you… I just… I'm really sorry.'

'I'm sure you are,' he bit out tersely.

Hearing the rustle of fabric, Poppy turned back to find him shoving the ends of his shirt into his trousers and swallowed hard. She wished she didn't know what lay beneath that shirt because she couldn't get the image of his toned torso out of her head. She watched, mute, as he straightened his cuffs and wound his red tie around his neck.

'At least the coffee missed your tie,' she offered.

His cutting glance told her more than words how little he thought of her comment. 'Is that supposed to make up for you dousing me with coffee?'

'I didn't *douse* you,' she said with a touch of asperity. 'You were rubbing my wrist while breaking up with your girlfriend.'

'And that made you spill coffee all over me?'

'I didn't do it deliberately,' she said, secretly thinking that actually he deserved it. 'Maybe you should be thankful it wasn't hot.'

His implacable gaze held hers. 'It was hot.'

Poppy bit her lip and watched with interest as he tussled with his tie. Cursing, he yanked it off and started over. Her lips twitched as her annoyance dissipated. There was something completely disarming about a man of his size and capability wrangling with an innocent strip of fabric. 'Do you want me to help you with that?'

Once more he flicked her with his green gaze. 'I think you've done enough, don't you?'

She held her hands up in front of her. 'Look—no coffee.'

Not even the trace of a smile crossed his sinful lips and she thought it such a shame that a man who was so good-looking should have no sense of humour.

Wondering if now might be the best moment for her to cut her losses she paused when he indicated to the computer open on his desk.

'Can you use a Mac?'

Hesitating only briefly she marshalled her usually sunny nature and smiled at him. 'Yes.'

'I need a report printed off before my grandfather arrives for a meeting. Think you can handle it?'

Poppy moistened her dry lips. 'Of course.' She sat down in his chair and set her fingers on the keyboard. 'What's the name of the file?'

He leaned forward and she got a delicious whiff of sandalwood cologne. 'If I knew that, intern, I'd already have it done, wouldn't I?'

'Oh, well, yes...' When she realised how close he was behind her Poppy's voice trailed off, her lips drying up again faster than a trickle of water in the Mojave Desert.

'It'll be something to do with Castiglione Europa, or CE for short,' he growled.

Ignoring the butterflies in her stomach Poppy scanned the folders on the screen and didn't see anything related to either of those. Then her eyes fell on an interesting one.

'Are you getting married?' she queried, peeking up at him.

'No.' He scowled. 'Why would you ask that?'

'No reason. Except Paula's got a file called "Operation Marriage" but that's probably got to do with the bet and not what you're looking for.'

'The *what*?'

Poppy told herself to shut up but knew by his thunderous expression that she was going to have to explain herself. 'The bet,' she said in an upbeat manner. 'Even I've heard that your grandfather is encouraging you to settle down—and, well... some of the legal department have dubbed it "Operation Marriage".'

His gaze turned flinty. 'I see the office grapevine is alive and well, then. Why have I not heard it?'

'Well, because the gossip is about you—obviously. But don't worry. Nobody thinks you'll do it.'

'Good to know my staff know me well at least.'

Poppy shrugged, relieved that he didn't seem annoyed by her revelation. 'I take it by your reaction you can't imagine anything worse than marriage?'

'Death.'

Poppy's smile grew at his grim tone. 'Right. But I think it's kind of sweet, actually. Your grandfather wanting you to find love.'

'I'm glad you think so.' He leaned over her. 'Click on the folder. Now open that file.' He pointed at the screen and Poppy had to force herself to focus on his instructions and not his steely arm brushing the outside of hers. 'There. Send that report to print.' He straightened away from the chair and cursed again.

Poppy glanced up to find him yanking his tie open again.

'I do know how to tie a tie,' she murmured.

His gaze told her he'd rather set his hair on fire than have her help him again.

'Fine.' His hands dropped to his sides and the two ends of the tie dangled down his lean body like twin arrows signalling paradise. 'I'm all yours.'

Sure that her face must look as hot as it felt Poppy reminded herself of the last man she had found attractive, and how that had ended for her and her brother.

Fortified by that particularly humiliating memory, she gripped the tie and reached up, doing her best to ignore the dark stubble that lined his hard jaw. He was tall, well over six feet, and she had to rise onto her toes to position the knot in the centre of his throat. This close, she could feel his heat, and smell his potently male scent. It made her want to lean in and nuzzle against him, to breath it in more deeply.

Not that she would. She wasn't a fool.

She noticed his tanned throat working as her fingers grazed his skin and she steadfastly refused to look at his face. 'What kind of knot do you want?' she asked, her voice husky and unlike the way it usually sounded.

'What kind of knots can you do?' His seemed deeper too, rougher.

'All of them.'

'All of them?'

Braving a quick glance upwards, she found that his eyes were heavy lidded as they met hers.

'Just how many are there?' he asked.

'Eighteen that I know of.'

'Eighteen.' His eyes glittered down into hers. 'Can you name them?'

'Yes. Do you want me to?'

'No.' He gave a short laugh. 'You've obviously done this before. Lucky guy.'

'Mannequin.' She adjusted the length of the tie and created a loop. 'I dressed in-store mannequins part-time during high school.'

His lips twisted into a small smirk. 'Lucky in-store mannequins.'

Poppy's hand flattened against his chest as the tie slipped. She could feel his heart beating heavy and strong beneath his breastbone... Was that a shudder that just went through his big body?

All of a sudden she felt surrounded by his warmth, his deliciously male smell, and she had to swallow hard before speaking. 'So, which one do you want?' she asked thickly.

'Just do a Windsor knot.' The words seemed to rumble out of his chest.

'That's the one most men prefer,' she said.

'Are you calling me common, Miss Connolly?'

'No.' Poppy tugged a length of the tie through another loop, her heart beating twice as fast as usual. 'It's just that it's the largest, and most men who wear neckties like to have a large knot.'

'Most women probably like them to have a large knot as well.' His voice was deep, his chest rising and falling evenly beneath her suddenly clumsy fingers. 'Wouldn't you agree?'

Deciding not to take this conversation any further for fear that he might actually be flirting with her, and it was the last thing she wanted, she concentrated on finishing the knot. 'I wouldn't know, Mr Castiglione. I don't date men who wear ties.' In fact she didn't date period.

'No?'

'No.'

'Then what do they wear?'

'Nothing. That is they…' Blushing furiously she folded his collar into place. 'There. All done.'

'A word of advice, Miss Connolly,' he began, waiting for her to look up at him before continuing. 'If you do happen to get a job here, don't ever hand me a call without first finding out who it is.'

Remembering how upset the woman on the end of the phone had been, Poppy pursed her lips. 'Not even if the person is crying?'

'*Especially* if the person is crying.'

Shaking her head Poppy wondered if he was really as ruthless and heartless as he was reputed to be. Of their own accord her eyes drifted to his mouth. His lips were firm and chiselled without seeming hard. Rumour also had it that he knew how to make a woman go wild in bed, and she wondered if his mouth would be rough or soft if she reached up and kissed him.

Instantly another fierce blush suffused her face as she registered the insanely inappropriate impulse, making her flustered. 'Why were you holding my wrist before anyway?' she asked belligerently. 'When you were on the phone?' He'd been stroking her skin so tenderly she could still feel the impression of his fingers against her skin.

'I don't really know.' His gaze flitted over her face, his green eyes hot and hungry. Poppy blinked, unable to look away. She was used to men noticing her, finding her attractive even, but she wasn't used to this answering heat rise up inside of her. She wasn't used to this overwhelming urge to…

'Scusa, Sebastiano, sono in anticipo?'

A deep, croaky voice intruded on the moment, startling Poppy out of her sensual haze.

CHAPTER TWO

HER BOSS WAS the first to step back and a floodgate of embarrassment rushed into Poppy's face. For a moment she had forgotten they were boss and employee. Forgotten that she was now late to meet Simon, who would be starting to fret when she didn't return when she said she would—a leftover issue from their childhood.

'No, you're not early, Nonno—in fact, you're late,' Sebastiano murmured, his eyes still on her. 'Miss Connolly was just helping me fix my tie.'

Feeling as if she'd just had her hand caught in the cookie jar, Poppy turned to face a much older version of her handsome boss and tried to smile.

His dark-green eyes were warm and encompassing as they swept over her.

'Nonno, this is Poppy Connolly. Poppy, this is my *nonno*, otherwise known as Signor Castiglione, or Giuseppe.'

'*Buongiorno, come stai?* Pleased to meet you.' His grandfather smiled broadly.

Still reeling from the shock of imagining how it would feel to kiss her boss—the owner of the company she at least needed a great reference from—Poppy murmured a greeting and wondered how rude it would be just to cut and run out the door.

About to suggest she do exactly that, her words were cut off when Sebastiano's mobile phone rang.

Glancing at the screen, he scowled. '*Nonno, scusa un momento.*'

Poppy wondered if it was his teary ex-girlfriend again,

but then realised that the poor woman probably didn't have his private mobile number or she would have rung it earlier instead of his office phone. It probably demonstrated her level of importance in the scheme of his life. Which was low. She wondered what a temporary girlfriend warranted at the end of an affair with the virile Sebastiano Castiglione? Diamonds or sapphires?

Shaking herself out of such senseless ruminating about a man who no doubt intended to put her on the black list with HR, Poppy smiled at his grandfather and once more tried to salvage something of the situation. 'Would you like a drink? Some coffee?' She tried not to cringe as she offered that. 'Or sparkling water?' That would be much better. No stains from sparkling water.

'No, no.' Signor Castiglione smiled. 'You relax.' He took a seat in one of the bucket chairs opposite the large oak desk. 'So, how long you know my grandson?'

'Oh, not long. About five weeks.' Or really, under an hour, if you counted face-to-face time.

'Ah, *va bene*. He is very demanding, no? He needs a firm hand.'

The image of someone handling Sebastiano Castiglione with a firm hand made Poppy want to laugh. But she fully agreed. 'Oh, absolutely.'

'But you handle him, *si*?'

Ah, definitely not *si*! She might have tied his tie before, but just being that close to him had completely tied her insides up in knots. 'I wouldn't say that exactly,' she hedged. 'Your grandson is his own boss.'

'Don't let him get his own way all the time. It is not good for him.'

He was telling her!

Poppy grinned at the lovely old man. 'I'll keep that in mind,' she murmured, thinking that there was little chance she'd even see her boss again after next week. If she even made it to next week. Especially after the way she'd just been caught staring at his mouth.

Mortified all over again, she stole a quick glance in Sebastiano's direction. Despite his less than stellar reputation with women, he was the most superb specimen of a man she had ever come across. Tall, broad-shouldered and with that air of power that was like an invisible warning to those who might dare to take him on.

Which would not be her. She was more a 'steer well clear of overpowering men' sort of girl. In fact, she was a steer well clear of *any* kind of men sort of girl. She had definite plans for the future, and they included climbing the corporate ladder, not falling for some good-looking, over-confident business mogul!

Unfortunately, before she could drag her gaze away from him, his eyes connected with hers and something hot and shivery jolted inside her. Once again sensing the effect he'd had on her, his eyes turned darker, his gaze telling her that he could read her most secret thoughts. The ones that said that he was so hot, she thought she might combust on the spot.

'Sei la persone giusta,' the old man said, nodding and smiling at her.

'What? Oh…yes.' Poppy turned to face him, relieved to have the unwanted spell of his grandson broken. 'Okay, well…' She moistened her lips and turned just as Sebastiano stepped forward, bringing them almost nose to chest. 'Sorry.' She stepped back quickly. 'I'll…uh…let you have your meeting. It was nice to meet you, Signor Castiglione.'

'What? No coffee?' Sebastiano mocked.

Poppy's eyes widened. *Was he making a joke?*

'Yes. It was a joke. Seems I'm a bit rusty. Thank you for tying my tie,' he said softly. Intimately.

'You're welcome.'

Cut and run! her common sense shouted at her. 'Have—

er—have a good meeting,' she said, finally kicking her brain into gear and hurrying through the office door. She didn't take another breath until the lift doors had closed around her and she could put that surreal experience behind her. Then she slumped against the wall and wondered if any of that had really happened.

As soon as she closed his office door, Sebastiano turned back to his grandfather. 'How was your flight?'

'Good. This woman.' He nodded slowly. 'I approve.'

An image of his intern's nimble fingers skating over his chest as she fixed his tie jumped into Sebastiano's consciousness.

He approved as well, or at least his body did.

From the first moment he'd looked round and seen her standing in his doorway he'd felt as if he'd been punched in the gut. It was why he had sounded so rude about her clothing. Of course she could wear casual clothing to the office on a weekend if she wanted. He wasn't a tyrant. He'd just been thrown by those velvet-blue eyes staring squarely back at him with no artifice in them at all.

The rest of her wasn't bad either. *Understatement*, he acknowledged wryly. Her figure was glorious: slim hips, rounded breasts pushing against her thin sweater and a thick pile of ash-brown hair pulled into a high ponytail, revealing a slender neck below sweet rosebud lips. She wasn't his usual type by a long shot but there was something about her that was at once innocent and impish. And hot. The way she had looked at him...an intelligent sparkle lighting those blue eyes as if she could see right through him.

When she had turned pink and asked him why he had been holding her wrist, he'd had an inexplicable desire to know what it would be like to wake up beside her, her face that colour from his love-making.

The memory pulled him up short. She was an intern in

his office so she was automatically off limits—no matter how tempting—and, even if she wasn't, he kept his relationships light and uncomplicated. Something about the way she hadn't turned coy or giggly to attract his attention told him that she was neither light nor uncomplicated. Which was why he intended to forget that he had even met her.

'I'm glad you approve,' he said to his grandfather. 'But it's your approval for me to take over as CEO of Castiglione Europa that I want. You can't keep travelling to Rome every other day to bark at everyone, and you know it. You also know that Nonna wants you to retire,' he added, playing his trump card. 'It's time.'

'Time to do what?' his grandfather grouched. 'Play *boules*? Pick grapes? Spend time with my grandchildren? Now there—' he pointed a knotted finger at Sebastiano '—there would be a reason to retire.'

And here were go, Sebastiano thought. *Operation Marriage*. It was a clever name for it but he'd still give Paula grief about not informing him of the office betting pool when she came in tomorrow morning. 'Yes, yes, I know what you want,' he said. 'And I'm working on it.'

'So what is the hold-up?' his grandfather asked. 'You are having trouble making her say yes, is that it?' His grandfather grinned, seeming to like that idea. But having a woman say yes wasn't a problem Sebastiano had ever encountered. Quite the opposite, in fact, but regardless of that he understood that he was too much of a loner to make any relationship work in the long term. A fact many of his women would be more than happy to attest to.

Realising that his grandfather was waxing lyrical about how nice Poppy seemed, Sebastiano shrugged off his uncharacteristic lapse in concentration. 'Forget all that,' he dismissed, not wanting to let his mind wander back to his sassy little intern. 'Tell me what I want to hear. You need to retire, and now, with this new deal I just finalised, the timing couldn't be better to merge SJC with the family business. You know it as well as I do.'

His grandfather steepled his hands beneath his chin, taking his time answering, as he was wont to do. When he was a child Sebastiano had grown fidgety under that steady regard—now he just used it himself when it suited him.

'I'll tell you right now, I'm impressed with what I just saw,' his grandfather said slowly. 'You should have mentioned Poppy sooner.'

Poppy? Were they still talking about his intern? 'Why would I mention her sooner?' he rasped, his brain prodding him that he was missing something important.

'Ah, I see, you want me to hand over the family company on your terms and not mine. That pride of yours will not do you any good in the long run, I've always told you that.'

'Nonno—'

'You always were a good boy, and now you have grown into a fine man. But seriously, Sebastiano, sometimes you cannot see what is in front of your face. Fortunately for you I am here to point out the obvious.'

Sebastiano frowned. 'Wait, do you...?'

His grandfather reached across the desk and laid a hand over his. His *nonno*'s skin was old and leathery, almost papery in its frailty, his fingers vibrating slightly as they gripped onto him. 'We have been waiting for you to ditch all those party girls and choose a nice girl to settle down with. And this girl is good.'

Sebastiano went perfectly still. His grandfather thought he and Poppy were an item—it was written all over his craggy features—which was ironic, when in fact they had only just met. But he supposed he could see how his grandfather had got that impression. For one, she had turned up in the office looking as much like an intern as he looked like a monk. And, two, he had very nearly lost his head and kissed her when she'd finished tying his tie.

'She is the one for you, and when your grandmother sees you together she will be so proud that we did right by you after all.'

Hold on—what? 'The one?'

'*Si*. And she said she knows how to handle you.' His grandfather chuckled. 'You need a strong woman like that.'

Sebastiano knew his grandmother ruled their *casa* but, hell, had Poppy—Miss Connolly—truly said she had him under the thumb?

His frown deepened; no wonder his grandfather had jumped to all the wrong conclusions. But why would she say that? And more importantly what was he going to do about it?

He recalled the slumberous way her eyes had moved over him when she'd been tying his tie. It had been from desire; he would have put money on it because his own body had sent the same message to his brain.

I want her, it had said, *right now*.

Sebastiano didn't want to think about his grandfather's reaction when he told him that, far from being his latest girlfriend, Poppy Connolly was nothing more than a temporary employee. But, instead of wasting his breath to try and convince the old man he was wrong, Sebastiano tried again to direct him away from his love life. 'Let's get down to business.'

'No. Let's save it for your trip to Italy.'

Sebastiano went as still as a stone. As a general rule he limited his trips to his home country as much as possible. Especially to the family *casa* where his memories were so strong. 'What trip to Italy?'

'For your grandmother and my sixtieth wedding anniversary. We are having a party. Bring your lovely Miss Connolly.'

Sebastiano couldn't move as his grandfather stood up. A look of sorrow briefly clouded his *nonno*'s eyes, his voice quiet when he broke the lengthening silence between them.

'We need to put the past to bed, *nipote mio*, and we want you to come. No more excuses. No more putting work first. It is time to move forward.' He cleared the emotion from his throat. 'After I tell Evelina about Miss Connolly she will want to meet her. In fact, I will text her now.'

Sebastiano blinked. 'Since when do you and Nonna text?'

'Since I bought her a smart phone for her birthday.'

His grandfather pulled his own phone out of his pocket and pressed the keys with the agility of someone half his age.

Sebastiano watched him, brooding. He would do a lot of things for his grandparents—he would even cast aside his deeply buried memories of the past to attend their anniversary—but pretend he had a relationship with a woman he barely knew and who might have just set herself up to become the next Mrs Castiglione?

Not a chance in hell.

CHAPTER THREE

'Two HUNDRED AND fifty thousand pounds?' Poppy stared at Sebastiano, who sat behind his desk like a leanly muscled King Tut with a pot of gold in front of him.

When he had requested to see her in his office she'd been convinced she was about to be fired. Instead he had offered her enough money to make her heart stop beating, in exchange for her pretending to be 'the light of his life', as he had condescendingly put it.

'As in two hundred and fifty thousand pounds *cash*?'

'You want more? Fine. Make it five hundred.'

Poppy's mouth was so dry it was arid. The man was insane. Or drunk. She narrowed her gaze, scanning his face for signs she was right. 'Have you been drinking?'

'Not since last night, and unfortunately the effects have worn off by now.'

She glanced around, waiting for a camera crew to jump out from behind his Chesterfield and yell, 'Surprise!' Only they didn't. All that happened was her heart thumped so fast she felt faint. 'I don't think this is very funny.'

'I never joke about money. And you only have yourself to blame.'

'Excuse me?'

'Something you said to my grandfather suggested that we were a couple. Something about handling me.' His dark brows rose mockingly. 'Which I can assure you, Miss Connolly, no woman will ever do.'

Poppy's throat felt tight and uncomfortable. 'I didn't say I could handle you.' She frowned. 'Your grandfather said something about you needing a firm hand and I agreed. Then he said something in Italian that I didn't get.'

'Do you remember what it was?'

She gave him a look. 'I grew up in the outskirts of Leeds, Mr Castiglione. My Italian starts with *si* and ends with *ciao*.'

'Well, thanks to my grandfather mistaking you for my latest mistress, it's about to extend to a few days on the Amalfi coast. So, what's your price?'

Poppy was so shocked at the thought that anyone could mistake her for this man's anything that she couldn't take any of this seriously. 'You're so desperate to impress him you're prepared to lie?'

'I like to think of it as taking advantage of an opportunity when it arises. And, believe me, I spent most of those wasted hours last night trying to come up with an alternative plan. I failed.' His sculpted mouth quirked at one corner. 'Something I don't admit to easily.'

Poppy let the subtle insult that he would rather do anything else than pretend he was in a relationship with her slide. She felt a little drunk herself at the thought of all that money. Five hundred thousand pounds? That kind of offer only happened in the movies, didn't it?

She stood up. 'I… I can't take your money.'

'Really? You'll do it for free?'

She heard the mockery in his tone and frowned. 'No, of course not, I—'

'Which is as I suspected. So, what is your price?'

'I'm not a prostitute,' she informed him sharply, those early schoolyard taunts about her biological mother coming back to haunt her.

'There's no reason to get in a temper,' he said calmly. 'I'm not suggesting we sleep together.'

Poppy scowled. 'Your arrogance knows no bounds, does it?'

'I'm a businessman, Miss Connolly, and I have a problem. Like it or not, you're my solution.'

'You're out of your mind.' Poppy shook her head. 'I won't do it.'

He regarded her steadily, making her feel hot in her navy suit. 'You're knocking back half a million pounds?' His toned was loaded with arrogant disbelief and it only made Poppy more determined to deny him. 'In *cash*.'

'I just…' She frowned. Growing up poor and without a proper family made a half a million pounds seem like a dream come true. 'It doesn't feel right.'

'It doesn't *feel* right?' She had no doubt that if he'd been a car he would have blown a head gasket by now. 'Are you seriously turning me down because it doesn't *feel* right?'

'I don't expect you to understand,' she shot at him, thinking of the devastated woman on the end of the phone the day before. 'You'd need to have *feelings* for that.'

'I have feelings,' he shot at her.

Poppy might have debated that but she still had a week left of her internship and she wanted to get a good reference—and, frankly, she felt a little dizzy. Five hundred thousand pounds was a lot of money. What she could do with it was mind-boggling.

Buy Simon new trainers, for one. The poor kid had been wearing hand-me-downs for as long as she had. But he was fifteen and the right trainers were integral to a teenager's self-esteem. With five hundred thousand pounds he would never have to go without anything again!

And five hundred thousand would be enough to help Maryann, whom she'd spent the rest of Sunday visiting. She'd also been researching MS on the computer to see if there was something she could do to help. Unfortunately the information had been depressing. Once the effects of the disease set in, Maryann would need a flat on the ground floor and, with no family or funds at her disposal, moving

was going to be difficult. Poppy had already thought of asking Maryann to move in with her and Simon, but Maryann
was as fiercely independent as Poppy was herself, so she
knew she wouldn't take to that idea easily.

But with half a million pounds Poppy might be able to
buy her a flat rather than have her continue to rent. She
could pay Maryann back for all the help she had given her
over the last eight years. Or could she? She had no idea how
far half a million pounds would stretch.

For a moment she was tempted to take the money, oh,
so tempted, but she knew there was no such thing as a free
lunch. Taking money for nefarious reasons would always
come back to haunt her. It would make her feel as cheap
as her beginnings.

'Well?'

Poppy felt a jolt go through her as Sebastiano impatiently
advanced into her personal space with the lazy grace of a
man who had it all.

'Well, what?' she asked, wishing she didn't sound so
breathless.

A muscle ticked in his jaw. 'Your answer?' he said in
his rich bedroom voice.

Holding her ground against his intimidating force, Poppy
shook her head. 'I'm not for sale, Mr Castiglione.'

'I know that.' He ran a hand through his hair. 'I'm not
asking for this to be real. It's a few days of your time. A
trip to Italy.' He pinned her to the spot with his stare alone.
'I'll even throw in a new wardrobe. No budget. It's every
woman's dream. Not to mention you could buy yourself
jeans that aren't about to fall apart.'

The fact that he had noticed her unfashionably worn
jeans made Poppy feel unclean. The fact that he was so arrogant, and thought he could buy anyone with his money,
made her even more resolved to hold her own against him.

'No.' Poppy stepped back from him, feeling immediately

cold without his body heat radiating close to hers. 'You'll have to find someone else.'

'Admit it,' he demanded quietly, his voice preventing her from turning around and walking out. 'You're tempted.'

'Of course I'm tempted,' she shot at him. He was *so* sure of himself. So sure of *her*. 'I wouldn't be human if I wasn't tempted, but...' She smoothed her already neat hair into place and noticed her hand was shaking. Turning it into a fist at her side, she raised her chin. 'I don't think I would like myself very much if I agreed to take your money to pretend to be something I'm not.'

Sebastiano blew out a beleaguered breath. '*Dio*, save me from martyrs.'

'I'm not a martyr.' She tilted her head back to glare up at him, wishing he wasn't quite so tall. 'I just have principles.'

He nodded and she felt that finally she'd penetrated his shallow exterior. It should have only taken the flick of her nail, given his lack of depth. Somehow finding out that he really wasn't a man of substance, but a self-absorbed rat like the rest of his ilk, had seriously disappointed her.

'Will that be all?' she asked stiffly, a picture of five hundred thousand pounds flashing like a neon sign inside her head.

Sebastiano stuck his hands in his pockets, his thunderstruck expression priceless. 'You're really turning me down?'

'Yes.' She tilted her chin higher, wondering if she wasn't being an idiot to do so. But then she thought about what she would have to do to get that money. Pretend to be this man's girlfriend. There was no way she could carry that off. Not for a million pounds!

His eyes gleamed predator-like as he watched her, and Poppy had the distinct impression she was in danger. *Run*, her inner voiced urged. So she did, reversing out of his office with the pace of a teenager texting on a phone.

When she was safely on the other side of the door she blew out a breath and walked on unsteady legs towards the lift. Since Paula's husband had indeed broken his ankle, she wasn't in the office, and Poppy was glad she didn't have to face the older woman's knowing gaze. Various employees had already warned her that every woman who came into contact with Sebastiano fell in love with him, and Poppy didn't want anyone to think that she had joined their adoring ranks when she hadn't.

Taking her phone from her handbag, she decided to duck into the ladies powder room before heading downstairs and facing her colleagues. She was tempted to call Maryann— Lord knew she could use the pep talk, and Maryann had been there for her right from the start. Well, not the start, exactly. Maryann had found her and Simon after Poppy had made the mistake of trusting a man that she shouldn't have. She had met him on the long train ride to London and somehow he had wheedled out of her that she was underage and that she and Simon were runaways with no place to stay.

At first Poppy had thought him a knight in shining armour. And he had been for two weeks. He'd been everything she could have asked for: complimenting her at every turn, giving them a place to stay and buying Simon little gifts. Then one night he'd come to her bedroom to extract payment for his many kindnesses, and when she'd refused he'd grown angry. He'd made her wake Simon and had turfed them both out into the wintry night, shouting that there was no one who would take her on anyway. Not with her 'idiot brother' in tow.

Finding out that he had stolen all her hard-earned savings was the lowest point and had shattered her trust altogether. Unable to go to the police for fear they would take Simon from her, they had been forced to slum it, sleeping in train stations and eating out of rubbish bins. Simon had only been seven at the time, to Poppy's seventeen, and she had cried silent tears every night, praying to God that an angel would come down and rescue them.

And one had. Without batting an eyelid, Maryann had taken them in, fed them, clothed them and given them the kind of affection they had missed out on for most of their early life. Through Maryann Poppy had learned real kindness and respectability and that was what she wanted for herself. For Simon.

But Maryann, who had lost her dear husband many years earlier, was a proponent of true love and would most likely ask Poppy all sorts of probing questions about her boss's offer that she'd rather not answer. Questions such as: *Is this the sexy boss whose photo you showed me? The one with more women than hot dinners? The one who makes you blush every time his name is mentioned?*

To which Poppy would have to answer yes, yes, and double yes.

She stared down at her phone and screwed up her nose. Probably best not to call her.

'Miss Connolly, are you in here?'

Poppy gave a small yelp when her boss's voice broke the heavy silence.

'Maybe.' She gripped her phone in both hands as if it were a sword, making no attempt to open the door.

'Are you planning to come out any time soon?'

Poppy rolled her eyes. Was it too much to ask to have a moment of privacy? 'Do I have to?'

'I prefer having conversations face-to-face. So, yes.'

'I thought we were done.'

'No.' He narrowed his eyes on her as she reluctantly opened the stall door. 'It ends when you say yes.'

'God, you're relentless. You should have been a barrister.'

He leaned his perfect butt against the basin, a killer grin

on his face, his muscular arms braced either side of his lean hips as if he was totally relaxed. *Yeah, right.*

'If that was supposed to be an insult, it failed,' he drawled. 'I respect people who go after what they want and succeed.'

'In other words, you're pushy.'

'Determined.'

Poppy rolled her eyes. 'You know you're in the ladies' loo right?'

His grin widened. 'I'm aware.'

'Well, I was having a private moment, and I'd like to go back to it.'

'It looks like you were about to have a meltdown. But you shouldn't. In my world women know what they want and go after it. It's nothing to be ashamed of.'

A shiver snaked down her spine. 'Why does that sound so cold?'

His half-smile turned mocking. 'I don't have a problem with it and I won't think badly of you for taking my offer.'

'You're all heart.'

'Actually, I'm all business.'

'Yes, well, it's an awful lot of money.'

'It isn't to me.'

Poppy shook her head. 'You could sound a little humble when you say that,' she said, a touch of exasperation in her tone.

'Why? It's the truth. I'm a wealthy man. That brings with it certain perks.'

'Like buying fake girlfriends.'

His green eyes glittered down into hers. He was too tall for her. His grandparents would notice that right away. 'I think I might have insulted you when I offered you five hundred thousand pounds,' he said.

Poppy blinked, hearing that figure again. Five hundred thousand was an amount of money she had never thought to see in one lump sum in her lifetime. The temptation to take it was wicked, and she finally understood those fairy tales where the hapless princess was lured to her doom by the evil villain. 'Yes, you did,' she murmured, holding firm to her flagging principles. 'Because I—'

'So I'm willing to up it to a million.'

'I am not— Did you just say a million pounds?'

He smiled at her smugly, victory lighting his green eyes. 'I did.'

Poppy stared at him blankly. She was sure that what he was offering must be immoral, and if she said yes she'd be looking over her shoulder for the rest of her life, expecting to see someone pointing a finger and accusing her of coming by the money unethically. It would be like being back at school all over again, when kids had whispered behind her back and called her 'Poor Poopy Poppy'. The memory put some much-needed steel in her voice. 'Stop. I already told you that I'm not for sale.'

His smiled dimmed and he stared at her for a long, tense minute before releasing a harsh breath. 'But you are exactly what I need. Okay, what do you want, then? What's your end goal?'

Poppy's head was spinning with so many pound signs she doubted she could even spell 'end goal' right now. She frowned. Did merely surviving each day count as an end goal? 'I don't really think in terms of end goals,' she said.

'Then you should start.' He paced away from her and glared at his reflection in the mirror with distaste. Or was that her reflection he was glaring at? 'Can we take this back to my office?' He held the door open for her, automatically expecting her to obey his request, his commanding demeanour suggesting that if she didn't he'd be happy to make her. 'The ladies' bathroom is hardly the place to have this conversation.'

Poppy stopped beside him. 'I'd rather not have this conversation at all.'

'I can see that. Be careful you don't knock yourself on the door.'

He steered her around the door she'd nearly walked into and Poppy found herself reluctantly seated on the opposite side of his desk before she thought better of it.

'So, if a lump sum is too difficult a concept for you to grasp, let's get to what it is that you do want.'

Too many things to count, Poppy thought, but none she would share with him. Especially not the number of wakeful hours she had spent last night reliving every hard angle of his torso. Sheesh! She had even imagined what it would have felt like if she had stretched up onto her toes and kissed him. 'I don't want anything.'

Sebastiano snorted at her prim response. 'That's patently untrue. Everyone wants something.' He glared at her. 'Even me. In fact, I find myself in the rare position of being a desperate man. So, what is it going to take, *bella*, to get you to give me one weekend out of your life to help an old man?'

Poppy's gaze sharpened. 'Is your grandfather unwell?'

'Would that influence your decision?'

Her frown deepened at the way he pounced on her unconscious show of sympathy. 'You would really use that as a bargaining tool?'

Sebastiano shrugged. 'If it would work.'

'You are such a shark!' Poppy exclaimed, both awed and shocked by his ruthlessness.

'Probably.' He sat forward, his green eyes intense on hers. Poppy's heart thumped heavily behind her breastbone. 'But my grandfather is old and I really don't know how much time he has left.' His lips firmed, as if that thought made him truly uncomfortable. 'And the old goat is far too stoic and proud to admit it if he were ill.'

Poppy heard the deep caring in those terse words. Perhaps it was Maryann being sick, and the dread Poppy felt at possibly losing her some time in the near future, but in that moment she felt an unexpected connection with her big, bad boss. Caring deeply, she knew, was an avenue for pain and she didn't wish that on anyone.

About to tell him that she understood how he felt, he undermined that feeling of accord with his next words.

'How about I grant you three wishes? Would that be more palatable to those prized principles of yours?'

'What are you, a genie now?' She snorted. The thought of seeing him wearing a turban and harem pants softened her irritation at his superior tone. 'Or my fairy godmother?'

'I'm hardly nice enough to be anyone's fairy godmother.'

'You got that right,' she agreed. 'You're a ruthless wolf.'

'I thought I was a shark.'

Poppy's lips twitched again. 'Shark... Wolf...' She swallowed as his gaze lingered on her lips. 'Anything with big teeth, really.'

The air between them suddenly pulled taut, and Poppy's mouth went dry as his smile kicked up at one corner. The man was devastating. Devastatingly attractive and devastatingly persistent.

'Think about it, Poppy,' he said, his soft tone and the use of her first name lending the moment an intimacy she didn't want to feel. 'Three wishes. Anything you want. If they are within my power to grant them, they are yours.'

She blinked in an attempt to shake off the spell he was subtly weaving around her. Three wishes did seem strangely more palatable than a cold, hard lump of cash, though she didn't know why it should, because in the end it would amount to the same thing.

He leaned forward, his gaze unwavering, a predator sensing weakness and homing in on the kill. 'People marry for money and status all the time. This is merely a weekend away. Nothing more.'

But it felt like more to her. She had never thought of her-self as someone who could be bought. Not when so many of her foster families had taken her and Simon in for the government grants they would collect, rather than wanting to offer them a secure home.

'Come on, Poppy,' he urged. 'Tell me something you've longed for lately.'

Love. Companionship.

She frowned. *Where had that come from?* She had her career to work towards. That was more important than a transitory state such as love.

'New shoes.' Distracted as she was by her own thoughts and his persuasive tone, she said the first thing that came into her head.

'New shoes?' A sexy grin crept across his face. 'Done. Name the designer and you can have a wardrobe full.'

'Nike, I think.'

'Nike?'

'Size ten.'

'You're serious?'

'Yes. Do you have a problem with that?'

'Okay, okay. Fine. Nike trainers. What else?'

'I don't know...' Suddenly her thoughts veered to Mary-ann. In particular to the issue of her needing a ground-floor flat. Like Poppy, she lived hand to mouth, and Poppy knew her lovely neighbour was scared about what the future held for her now.

'A new apartment,' she said, waiting for her boss to laugh and tell her she was dreaming.

'Now you're speaking my language,' he said, confidence oozing from every pore. 'A penthouse, no doubt. How many bedrooms?'

'It can't be a penthouse, they're on the top floor.'

'I'm well aware of where a penthouse is located,' he said. 'I own several.'

Poppy was so deep in thought she barely heard him. 'It has to be on the ground floor. And near Brixton.'

'Brixton?'

'Yes. Maryann is really attached to Brixton.'

'Maryann?'

'My neighbour.' The more she thought about it, the more she warmed to the idea. 'And it should be near a park and the tube. Maryann likes to go into Stratford most Saturday afternoons. Her husband is buried there.'

'Right.' He pinched the bridge of his nose. 'I'm getting a headache just thinking about it. Give the details to HR.'

'I'm not giving the details to HR!' Poppy exclaimed. 'It will completely ruin my professional reputation before I've even got one.'

'Fine, send me an email. But what does your neighbour have to do with this anyway?'

'The apartment is for her.'

'I thought it was for you.'

'She needs it more than I do.'

He looked at her as if she'd suddenly grown two heads. 'Okay, fine, whatever. And the last one?'

Poppy stared at him, realising too late that in negotiating with him she was entering into a deal she wasn't at all sure she wanted to make. A deal with the devil. 'I…eh… I don't have a third.' Mostly because her brain had now turned to mush.

'Nothing for yourself?'

Those first two *were* for her. For her peace of mind. She shook her head, trying to clear her thinking. What was she doing even considering this?

'No need to stress,' he said, once more reading her correctly. 'When you think of it, you let me know. In the meantime we will leave for Italy at the end of the week.'

'I don't have a passport!'

'I'll take care of it. And Poppy?'

She raised troubled eyes to his. 'Yes?'

He came around his desk all lean, hard, muscular grace. 'Thank you.'

He held out his hand and guided her to her feet. Poppy felt a tingling sensation light up her arm at his touch, distracting her. 'Wait!' she cried. 'The end of the week? That's too soon. I can't get organised by then.' Meaning that she couldn't organise care for Simon by then.

'You'll have to. That's when my grandparents are holding their anniversary party.'

'Anniversary party?' Her stomach pitched alarmingly. 'This gig just gets better and better.'

'My grandparents are very important to me. Please remember that.'

'So how can you lie to them so easily?' she asked, hoping to see some faint trace of humanity in him.

He shrugged, giving her nothing. 'I see this more as an opportunity to get an outcome that is long overdue.'

'You running your family business.' Him making even more money.

'Yes.'

He really was a shark, Poppy thought, a shark who swam around in shallow waters. What was she doing getting mixed up in this? 'Can't you tell them we broke up and take one of those breathtaking blondes you apparently date instead?'

'No.' His jaw hardened. 'My grandfather has it in his head that you are "the one" for me, and no blonde, no matter how breathtaking, will cut it.'

What didn't cut it for Poppy was how attracted she was to him. He was a shining example of how little taste her hormones truly had when it came to choosing men. 'Don't you find this all a bit deceptive?' she pleaded.

Sebastiano's lids came down to shutter his gaze. 'Your point?'

'My point is that you don't seem to care.'

She wasn't sure she'd kept the distaste from her voice when he scowled. 'What I care about right now is taking over CE.'

'So you believe that the end justifies the means?'

'When it fits.'

Just like the well-dressed louse who had picked her up. But this wasn't the same thing, was it? She had her wits about her this time. And this man was granting her three wishes, not trying to take something from her.

'Poppy?'

She bit her bottom lip, and, when her eye finally lifted to his, his were softer. 'I can see this is not as easy for you as I thought it would be—but my grandfather needs to retire. If him believing I am in love with you achieves that, then I'm willing to bend the truth a little.'

Poppy's eyebrows rose. 'A little?'

He smiled. 'A lot.'

Something in his tone told her that the deception wasn't as easy for him as he made out. Maybe it was that, or maybe it was just the fact that she could already see the expression on Simon's face when he received his new trainers—not to mention Maryann's delight when she learned she would be moving into a ground-floor flat beside a park—but Poppy found herself oddly compelled to agree. 'Okay.' She released a long, drawn-out breath. 'I'll do it.'

He gave her a faintly mocking smile. 'That face is not going to convince anyone you think I'm the love of your life.'

'That's because I feel sick,' she said.

As sick as she used to feel whenever the social worker would turn up and tell her that she and Simon were moving on to yet another family. She had that same dreadful sense that her life was headed over a cliff and she had no idea if the landing would be soft or hard, experience warning her to prepare for the worst.

Sebastiano shook his head. 'I'm not sure you're actually real.'

Poppy grimaced. 'Well, that makes two of us, because I'm not sure you are either. Now, if you'll excuse me, I have to get my head around a presentation for Mr Adams. Oh, and feel free to change your mind about all this. I won't be sorry.'

'I won't change my mind.'

Long after the building had emptied for the day, Sebastiano sat in his office, staring across at Big Ben but not really seeing it. He couldn't quite believe he had just coerced a woman into posing as his fake lover, or how difficult it had been to get her to agree.

Honestly, he'd expected the whole process to take no more than five minutes. Offer her a large sum of money and count the seconds until she said yes. When Poppy had baulked he had initially believed she'd been holding out for more money. No surprise there. What *had* been a surprise was how hard he'd had to work to convince her, and how heated his blood had become in the process. He knew it was just ego, but still the whole time she had been resisting him that voice in his head had said, *Take her!* and *Now!* with predictable consistency.

A voice he would not be listening to next weekend. Sebastiano had met enough women on the make to encourage a lifetime of bachelorhood. Women who would do and say just about anything to marry up in society. Since he was from a centuries-old Italian dynasty with all the trappings that entailed, he'd been a target for avaricious types ever since he'd reached puberty.

But he wouldn't be caught. And not just because he distrusted most of the women he met, but because his life was perfect as it was. Why interfere with that?

A pair of bold velvet-blue eyes slid into his consciousness. Was Poppy Connolly for real? He didn't think so, but he wasn't going to waste time wondering about it. She had agreed to go with him and that was all there was to it.

He blew out a breath and pushed to his feet.

In truth he didn't need to take her to Italy with him. Yes, it would be easier to present the package his grandfather believed to get what he wanted, but it wasn't essential. He hadn't even confirmed that his grandfather was right in his assumptions.

He could easily turn up to the villa alone and they could laugh at the mistake over a *negroni* or two. Sebastiano could then assure his grandfather that he was perfectly fine as he was, and wear the old man down without having to revert to a lie.

The problem was that he still remembered how soft the skin was on the inside of Poppy's wrist, and he'd enjoyed meeting a woman who hadn't behaved as if he was the best thing since sliced bread.

His lips twisted into a self-mocking smile. Was it just the novelty of having a woman say no to him? Surely he hadn't become that arrogant, or full of himself?

Or was it the thought of returning to his family home at this time of the year, alone?

Yes, that made his stomach knot, but it had been fifteen years since the accident. And, while he might still live with the guilt and loss, it didn't govern his actions any more. He'd mastered that years ago. Hadn't he?

Perhaps it was nothing more than simple lust. He'd felt it straight away, an edgy hunger to feel her against him. Feel her against him and under him and over him. Feel every soft, satiny, naked inch of her as he buried himself deep inside her. Just the thought of it aroused him to a burning point of hardness. Which was ridiculous in the extreme. His libido did not control him. He controlled his libido.

Regardless, this relationship was fake, he reminded himself, one-hundred-percent fake. And that made Poppy Connolly one-hundred-percent off limits.

CHAPTER FOUR

'WHERE DID YOU say you were going?'

'I didn't,' Poppy signed back to her brother, debating between packing black linen dress trousers that had seen better days or a navy skirt that was a little on the short side. 'But it's somewhere in Italy. I was planning to text you the details after I arrived.'

Black trousers definitely. She didn't want to give Sebastiano Castiglione any ideas that this relationship was anything other than phony.

'Italy!' Her fifteen-year-old brother signed excitedly, bouncing up and down on the bed as if he'd just been stung by a wasp. 'I want to come.'

'You can't,' she signed. 'I already told you, it's a work thing, and I deliberately didn't tell you where I was going because I knew you'd want to come.' She went to smooth his fringe back from his face like she'd used to when he was little but he moved back out of range. 'You know I'd love to take you. Don't make me feel guilty.'

'I won't if you at least let me stay in the flat by myself.'

Poppy pressed her two fingers to her thumb to signal no. 'You have to stay with Maryann. And make sure you heat up the Bolognaise I prepared for dinner tomorrow night. I don't want her having to do any cooking this weekend.'

Her brother gave her a belligerent stare. 'I'm old enough to stay by myself.'

'You're fifteen.'

'Exactly.'

Poppy sighed. 'If you don't leave now you'll be late for

school,' she signed to him. 'And stay off your phone this weekend. You need to read a real book instead of playing games all the time.'

'I tell you what...' He uncoiled his lanky frame from the bed, signing rapidly. 'I'll read a real book if I can stay here by myself.'

Poppy grabbed a couple of tops that went with the black trousers. 'Go to school.' She pulled him in for a kiss. 'I love you.'

He gave her the shorthand sign for 'love you' in return before blowing out of the door like a dervish in his new trainers. Or one of the ten pairs of new Nike trainers! They had arrived the day after she had struck her devil's pact with Sebastiano and Poppy had been forced to say she had won them in a work raffle to explain the extravagance.

She didn't know if Sebastiano's generosity was a sign of the man himself, or just his desperation to get his own way. Somehow she suspected the latter.

Straightening her bed, she padded into the bathroom and took a shower. It was still a few hours until Sebastiano was due to arrive, but she felt jittery.

Around noon she received a phone call from her brother. Usually they used messaging, but due to a new hearing app she was able to speak into the phone and have her words converted to text. Simon wanted to know if he could go to the movies that afternoon with some friends he had made at his new school and Poppy's heart swelled. Because her brother had been born deaf he'd had many developmental delays and those, combined with their volatile childhood, had seen him become a shy and insecure kid. Lately, though, he seemed to be coming out of his shell and it made Poppy's heart sing to see it.

Telling him it was fine with her, she jumped when a decisive knock sounded at her front door. Knowing who it would be, she told Simon she loved him before opening the door wide, all her nerves from earlier returning full force at the sight of her boss standing in her dank hallway.

He was so tall, dark and utterly male he took her breath away. It just wasn't fair that a man should look this good and yet have no decent moral fibre about him. The reminder of his poor character had her determined that she would not let him walk all over her.

'Are you early, or am I late?' she asked, raising her chin in an unconscious challenge.

'I'm on time,' he drawled. 'But if you're like every other woman I know, you'll be late.'

Poppy's eyes narrowed. 'For the sake of our very fake relationship I'm going to pretend you didn't say that.'

Sebastiano laughed. 'Are you going to invite me in or are we going to conduct this conversation in the hallway?'

'Better than the ladies' toilets.'

A small smile tugged at the corner of his mouth. *'Touché.'*

He brushed past her as he entered her tiny hallway and Poppy's eyes unconsciously drifted to the shape of his butt in the denim jeans he wore. Combined with the effect of the thick navy sweater and black boots, he looked good enough to eat. Not that she was hungry.

'Coffee?' she offered pleasantly.

His gaze, that had been scanning her shabby living room with laser like intent, swung back to hers. 'Cute, but I think we should skip the refreshments. Who were you on the phone to just then?'

He asked the question as if he had every right to know and Poppy's hackles immediately rose. It was instinctive for her to shield her brother from prying, ridiculing eyes and a deep sense of self-preservation told her that the less this man knew about her life, the better.

'Nobody,' she said.

'It didn't sound like nobody.'

Knowing he wouldn't let up until he had the information he wanted she relented. 'It was Simon, if you must know.' And she wasn't revealing any more than that.

His mouth firmed as he noted her belligerent expression but he didn't push. 'Are you ready to go? My plane is waiting.'

His plane was waiting?

She already felt incredibly inept standing before him in a cheap corduroy skirt, an even cheaper blouse and second-hand boots. 'Hold up a minute, my lady's maid is still packing my trunk.'

His lips quirked. 'Do I sense some hostility, Miss Connolly?'

Poppy huffed out a breath. 'Not really. More a change of heart.'

He glanced at her feet. 'What, the trainers didn't fit?' He scrunched his brows together. 'I have to confess I'm struggling to picture size-ten trainers on those feet. Or is it that your neighbour wasn't happy with the apartment she was shown yesterday. Is that the problem?'

Poppy shoved her hands on her hips and glared at him. Maryann had come to her late last night in a whirlwind of excitement with news that, out of so many MS patients, she had been singled out to receive a grant to cover all her medical expenses, as well as assistance to move to a ground-floor apartment beside a park. She had kept pinching herself the whole time and didn't know how she could have been the recipient of such good luck.

Poppy had told her that of course she deserved every ounce of that luck, and more, to which Maryann had said that Poppy's luck was changing as well.

'I can feel it.' Maryann had hugged her tight. 'It started when you got that coveted internship. You're such a smart, wonderful girl, Poppy, and a beautiful sister to Simon.'

Poppy's eyes had welled up and she now thought it completely heartless of Sebastiano to remind her of that part of their deal right when she was trying to figure out how to back out of it.

'She loved it,' she informed him with a sigh. 'And thank you for arranging to have her put on the special list for the new drug trials. That was...thoughtful.'

'You're welcome.'

'But I still think this is a bad idea, Mr Castiglione.'

'You cut a deal,' he said with ironclad resolve. 'And the name is Sebastiano, or Bastian. I answer to both.'

But which did he answer to in bed?

Horrified by that rogue thought, Poppy pressed her sweaty palms together. Therein lay one of the reasons this was a bad idea: she hadn't been able to stop thinking about Sebastiano all week. In particular, his impressive naked chest! It made her feel less in control to be at the whim of someone else and she didn't like it. And she hadn't felt like that for a long time.

Not since she'd picked herself up as a lost seventeen-year-old and decided she would never be at another person's mercy again. And it wasn't so much that she felt out of control right now, it was more that she felt...okay *out of control*. Totally out of control. And inferior, if she was being completely honest with herself. Lacking, in some way. It would take his family two seconds at most to realise she was an imposter.

Especially when his family was descended from centuries-old Italian royalty. 'They'll see right through me,' she implored. 'They'll know we're a sham.'

'Just relax, Poppy, I have this.'

'But how can you?' she asked.

'I arrange multi-billion-dollar business deals all the time. Pretending that we're a couple will be a walk in the park by comparison.'

She wished she agreed, but she did not arrange multi-billion-dollar deals at all, so for her this was much worse.

'You'll really do anything to get control of this company won't you?' she said.

'Yes.'

'Surely your grandfather knows that.'

'In my experience people see what they want to see. My grandfather wants me to fall in love. Since that's his focus, that's what he believes has happened.' He paced around her small living room. 'Sometimes I think I should have just bitten the bullet—isn't that what you English would say?—and taken a wife already.'

His cavalier attitude to something Poppy had romantically believed—hoped—led to happy ever after for some people appalled her. 'It's not too late,' she drawled. 'Perhaps you could send Paula out to Fortnum and Mason's to pick one up for you this afternoon. Who knows, you might even find one on sale.'

Sebastiano cast her an amused glance. 'There's that latent hostility again, Miss Connolly.'

'What you just said was completely outrageous,' she snapped. 'One doesn't just bite the bullet and get married. But why haven't you, out of interest? Is it that you don't believe in love or because no woman would have you?'

Sebastiano gave her a mocking smile. 'I'm not married because I don't care to be married. But I'm sure love exists. In fact, I know it does, because I've seen it. I just don't want it or need it for myself. My life is perfect as it is.'

'Your grandfather doesn't think so.'

'My grandfather is old-world Italian. To him, family is life.'

'And what about your parents? Are they happily married?'

A muscle ticked in his jaw. 'My parents are dead and

therefore off limits as a topic for discussion. Any other questions?'

Immediately contrite by the wealth of hurt she picked up in his aggravated tone, Poppy's own irritation fell away. What did she care what he thought about love and marriage? It wasn't as if this was real. Surreal, maybe. But definitely not real.

'Now I just feel bad,' she said. 'But if this is supposed to look legitimate then we would know certain things about each other. Like how they died.'

His green eyes turned as murky as the waters at Loch Ness on a stormy day. 'They died in a car accident. I was fifteen.' He paced her small room like an angry caged tiger. Or panther. He was more panther, with his dark good looks and green, green eyes. He swung those eyes to her now and once more she felt the jolt of a strange connection in her chest. For a minute neither of them spoke, then his lips twisted in a wry grimace. 'Satisfied?'

No, she wasn't satisfied. He had been around the same age as Simon when his parents had died and she knew how devastated Simon would be if something were to happen to her. The realisation made her want to go to Sebastiano, wrap her arms around him and keep him safe from the harsh realities of the world. Which was absurd. Not only would he not welcome her efforts, but if there was anyone who could take care of themselves in this world it was this man.

She felt a little sick at having pried into his life. Lord knew there were things she didn't want him knowing about her life. 'I'm sorry for your loss,' she said. 'I didn't mean to upset you.'

'You didn't,' he bit out, running his hand through his hair and giving it that sexily mussed look she didn't want to find attractive. 'You've worked for my company for six weeks, so you already know everything you need to know about me. If you want my favourite colour or my favourite food, the answer is blue and *pesto alla genovese*.'

'You're that complex, huh?'

His grin was slow. 'I do have a voracious sexual appetite, but I doubt my grandparents will quiz you about that.'

Poppy shook her head. 'TMI,' she said, making him laugh softly.

'So, what about you?' he asked.

The simple question made her instantly wary. 'No, I do not have a voracious sexual appetite.'

Her cheeks stung with embarrassment, worsening when his lips kicked up at one side. 'Are you sure?'

'Yes!'

'Pity,' he drawled meaningfully. 'But I was referring to you as a person. You drilled me about my life: turnabout is fair play.'

Poppy swallowed heavily, even more embarrassed than before. 'Red and rice pudding,' she said stiffly.

Sebastiano shook his head slowly. 'You're going to have to do better than that, *bella*.'

Noting her red face Sebastiano decided to cut her a break and moved to the roughly sanded sideboard against the cracked wall, studying the meagre number of photos on display. There was one of Poppy a few years younger, with a young boy and an older woman, and various others that were a variation on the same theme.

'Who's the boy?'

'My brother.'

Sebastiano cast her a glance over his shoulder, noting her stiff shoulders and pursed lips. So Little Miss Intrusive didn't like being on the receiving end of probing questions. How interesting.

Not that he really cared. He already knew her impressive academic credentials and he had no wish to learn more about a woman he found himself unwittingly attracted to and would never see again after the weekend.

But she did have a point. If this were a legitimate relationship they would know certain things about each other. Things his grandfather, in particular, would expect him to know.

'So this woman would be your mother, yes?' He pointed to a framed photograph, curious despite his intentions to remain detached from her.

'No.' She came to stand beside him and he could smell the faint trace of flowers clinging to her skin. He doubted it was perfume, because she didn't seem the type, so it had to be soap. And her. He inhaled deeply, his gaze drifting to her straight hair hanging past her shoulders in a thick, lustrous curtain. It looked soft to the touch and he had to shove his hands inside his pockets to stop himself from finding out for sure.

When she didn't elaborate on her answer about the woman in the photo, he raised an eyebrow. 'Just "no"?'

She sighed. 'That's Maryann. My neighbour with MS.'

'And your parents?'

'They're not around.'

'Where are they?'

'I don't think it's fair that you get to ask me all sorts of probing questions,' she complained, 'when you gave me such clear back-off signals before.'

'I answered your questions, didn't I? Now you answer mine.' He scowled down at her. 'Anyway, you were right, my grandfather will expect me to know everything about you.'

Her eyebrows climbed her forehead. 'Everything?'

'Yes. The Castiglione men are very protective of what is theirs. If I was truly in love with you, I would know everything about you.'

Even as he said the words, Sebastiano knew he was

being unfair but he didn't care. This was just strategising to achieve the best outcome. And he was a master strategist.

He wasn't sure she was going to answer, but then she said, 'My mother died of a drug overdose when I was twelve and I—I don't remember my father.'

Shocked by her matter-of-fact revelation, Sebastiano stared down at the top of her glossy head. 'Who raised you and your brother?'

'We lived in the foster care system until I was seventeen.'

Foster care?

'It wasn't as bad as you probably imagine,' she said, reading him correctly, and Sebastiano knew by her off-handed tone, and the way she avoided eye contact, that it had probably been very much worse than anything he could imagine. 'So we're both orphans,' he mused.

She gave him a look. 'So it seems. Hell of a thing to have in common.'

He paused, noting the way her chin jutted forward, as if she dared him to feel sorry for her. 'You're a tough little thing, aren't you, Poppy?'

Her small chin jutted even further forward in a stubborn tilt. 'I thought your plane was ready to go, Mr Castiglione?'

For a moment there was something naked on her face— pride? Determination? Vulnerability?—before she quickly masked it. Sebastiano felt a stab of admiration for her. This place she lived in might be small and run-down, but she'd made it a home, and it struck him that for all its negatives it was probably far more welcoming than any one of the show pieces he lived in. And why that bothered him he didn't know.

'It's Sebastiano,' he reminded her, watching as she crossed the room and disappeared through a door. She returned a moment later carrying a worn duffle bag.

His eyes narrowed on the bag. 'That's all the luggage you're taking?'

'Afraid so,' she said. 'Justina broke the trunk.'

'Justina?'

'My lady's maid.'

'Ah…' He shook his head. His grandfather was right; this woman had a rod of steel running through her. And yet she looked as delicate and as untouched as a hothouse flower. 'It's hard to get good help nowadays,' he agreed.

Her soft lips curled into a reluctant smile, as if she hadn't expected him to play along with her joke. 'You're telling me.'

Then her gaze drifted from his and she looked so lost and alone he felt an inexplicable need to comfort her. An inexplicable need to take her into his arms, stroke her hair back from her face and tell her that whatever, or whoever, had dimmed the brightness in her beautiful blue eyes would find themselves on the wrong side of his wrath. Then he wanted to do what he'd wanted to do since he'd walked in and kiss the breath from her body.

He didn't know what it was about her that drew him but there was no denying it existed. Or that he would have to control it. What was between them was business, not pleasure.

'Are you ready?' he asked, clearing the gruffness from his voice.

'Ready as I'll ever be. Bring on the weekend!' She picked up her bag and pasted a wide smile on her face.

Sebastiano walked over and took the bag from her. It barely weighed enough to be holding socks. 'Try not to look like you're going to the gallows, *bella*; I promise you, everything will be fine.'

'You know, you shouldn't make promises you can't keep.'

'Who said I can't keep this one?'

She gave him a superior look. 'Sorry, I forgot, you eat billion-dollar business deals for breakfast.'

Sebastiano couldn't hold back a laugh, inexplicably delighted by this prickly female he just couldn't get a bead on. 'I don't eat them, *cara*, I make them.'

She rolled her eyes, something no woman had ever done to him before, and grabbed her winter coat. She shrugged into it, the fabric of her shirt pulling tight across her small, high breasts. His groin hardened and he immediately tamped down on the reaction before following her to the door. A sense of foreboding warned him that the weekend might not go as easily as he had first hoped.

CHAPTER FIVE

POPPY STARED OUT of the window as Sebastiano's private jet levelled out above puffy white clouds floating in a perfect blue sky. The tranquillity of the view did not at all reflect the myriad of troubled emotions swirling around inside her.

She couldn't quite put her finger on what was bothering her but Sebastiano's words—that if he were in love with her he'd know everything about her—had unfurled something deep inside her.

Nursing a cup of coffee the stewardess had just handed her, the words played over and over in her mind. She had never had anyone other than Maryann take a genuine interest in her, and in many ways that had been a good thing. Having had a mother who had either been borderline unconscious or just plain absent, it had fallen to Poppy to care for her infant brother and the experience had taught her how to take care of herself. How to take care of her own.

Unfortunately it hadn't taught her how to pretend to be in love with a man she hardly knew. A man who until today had been her boss. She screwed up her nose. Not only had she never seen a healthy adult relationship, she had never been particularly good at pretending. It was partly why she and Simon had been shipped around between so many families on a semi-regular basis.

'There's just something about her,' she had overheard one of her foster mothers say. 'We can't explain it.'

'She looks at you with them big, innocent blue eyes of hers…makes a person feel guilty,' another had said. 'And that brother of hers? I didn't know he was retarded when I agreed to take them on.'

'Now you listen, girl,' a particularly obnoxious foster father had warned, pointing a finger in her face. 'When that effing social worker turns up, you make like everything is sweet. You do that and it will work out real good for you and your baby brother.'

Poppy felt that old tightness grip behind her breastbone. She knew now that the social worker had done her a huge favour in removing her and Simon from that particular family, but it didn't diminish that old sense of failure she struggled to shake off. That old sense that the world was a harsh place and it was every man for himself.

And now she had to pretend she was in love with a man she was stupidly attracted to, but one who was a virtual stranger. At least on a personal level. And what if she failed? Would Sebastiano withdraw the help he had already started to give Maryann? Would he take back Simon's new trainers?

It was hard for Poppy to trust anyone, let alone a man known for his ruthless exploits, and she knew that part of her anxiety about the weekend was in knowing that she was putting herself in the way of a man who could make an unguarded woman do stupid things. Stupid things such as fall in love with him and cry over the telephone when he ended their relationship.

Not that she was in any danger of falling in love with him—that kind of thing didn't happen after only meeting someone a week ago—but she couldn't deny that a part of her was intrigued by him. And not just because he was the sexiest man she had ever seen. It was his self-confidence and, yes, as much as she didn't like to admit it, his arrogance. He was just so sure of himself, it automatically made her feel safe in a way she never had before. Then there was the way he looked at a woman. As if he knew all the ways to touch her and give her more pleasure than she could ever dream about. And that he'd enjoy doing it. Now, *that* was definitely appealing!

Poppy had never experienced any sort of passion, hence her virgin status, but when Sebastiano looked at her with those knowing emerald-green eyes she wanted him to do things to her. She wanted him to reach for her and put his hands on her, as she had imagined him doing the other day in his office. She wanted to run her hands through the mat of hair on his manly chest and press her aching body against his until she couldn't think of anything else.

She shifted in the soft leather seat, an uncomfortable heat flaring between her thighs.

Even if he saw her in a remotely similar light, she wouldn't want anything to happen between them. Unfortunately, to a man like Sebastiano she would just be another fish swimming in his very large ocean, one he would cast off as soon as he'd had his fill of her. Anyway she couldn't afford to be distracted from her goals by a man who was only out for a good time.

She glanced at him working in the seat near the front of the plane. She should also be going over study notes for an exam she had to sit in a couple of weeks, so she pulled her ancient laptop out of her satchel even though she doubted she'd take in a word.

The problem was that she had responsibilities. A teenaged brother to take care of, and a plan to be top of her class so that she could get any job she wanted straight out of university. She didn't need a man to derail her or, worse, weaken her. That had been her mother's plight and it wouldn't be hers.

And yet here she was, mooning over a man who broke hearts like they were china at a Greek wedding. She scowled at her notes. She wasn't mooning, exactly, she was… She was… She sighed, her mind turning to the three wishes he had promised her. Accepting his deal came too close to relying on someone else for her liking, though at the same time she couldn't deny that he had thrown her a lifeline. That was if he kept his word—and so far it certainly seemed as if he would. And that was another thing. She wasn't used to that kind of follow-through from anyone other than Maryann and it made her feel jittery because deep down she knew it was most likely too good to be true.

She sighed. If only she didn't feel so conflicted when she was around him. On the one hand, she wanted to push against all that dominant male energy to find the flaws in his armour, and on the other she wanted to lean into it and hope that there were no flaws. She wanted to lean into it, soak him up and learn what it felt like to be cherished by someone who would love her enough that he would want to know everything about her.

The latter being the most dangerous inclination of all, and one she could never afford to give in to.

'Poppy?'

Startled out of her reverie, Poppy glanced up, not realising that Sebastiano had come to sit beside her. Immediately her nerves tightened and the blood fizzed in her veins. Forcing out a slow, relaxed breath, she collected herself. 'Yes?' she queried mildly.

'I have something for you.'

Poppy stared at the oblong-shaped blue velvet box. 'What is it?'

'A gift to show you my appreciation,' he drawled. 'Open it.'

Reluctantly she did and gaped at him when she saw a stunning, luminous pearl surrounded by diamonds. 'This is the most beautiful thing I've ever seen.'

Pleased, glittering green eyes stared down at her. 'I'm glad you like it. I think it will look perfect against your skin.'

Poppy stared at the jewels that twinkled under the plane's halogen lights, her heart beating too fast. No wonder women fell for him hook, line and sinker. Rich, good-looking, generous and *entitled*, she reminded herself.

'Please tell me these are fake.'

Sebastiano smiled. 'I don't do fake.'

Her eyebrows hit her hairline and she saw that he had immediately picked up on her train of thought.

'Jewellery. I don't do fake jewellery,' he amended.

Poppy closed the box before she became too dazzled to give the precious jewels back. 'If I wore these, I'd be mugged.'

'You will if you continue to live in the neighbourhood you're in now.' He frowned. 'I hope that third wish you're holding on to includes a new home somewhere more salubrious.'

He hadn't tried to keep the contempt out of his voice and it raised her hackles. 'Not everyone can be born rich.'

'I know that. But I'm giving you a chance to improve yourself.'

'Oh, really?' It was all Poppy could do not to tell him what he could do with his chance. 'Why thank you, kind sir.'

He sighed and ran a hand through his hair. 'That wasn't what I meant and you know it.'

He suddenly looked tired and Poppy suspected he was as tired as she felt. She knew from the legal team that he'd had back-to-back meetings all week and maybe their current situation had played on his mind more than he let on. Or maybe that was just her imagination going wild, and the dark circles beneath his eyes were because he'd followed back-to-back meetings with back-to-back sex.

'I admit my neighbourhood isn't brilliant,' she said, forcing herself to be conciliatory. 'But it's not that bad either.'

'I suspect you know how to make the best of a bad situation, *bella*. But I saw a group of teenage boys working the corner of your apartment block and they weren't selling lemonade.' He smiled once more, as if everything was right with his world, and no doubt it was. It was just hers that had become topsy-turvy.

'They're okay if you leave them alone.' She handed back the velvet box. 'Thank you, but I can't take this.' She sounded ungracious, and she hadn't intended to, but she was a little disconcerted at his insight into her personality. She usually did try to make the best of bad situations.

'Why can't you take it?'

'Well, for a start I believe this is usually the kind of thing you give *after* the relationship has ended; and for another it won't suit my complexion.'

'I bought it to suit your complexion.'

He had bought it? Not Paula?

'Well, there you go.' Her throat felt tight. 'You do fall short on some things. I'll alert the press. I can see the caption now: *Sebastiano Castiglione, megalomaniac, human after all.* It'd sell a few papers, don't you think?'

'What I think is that you have a very smart mouth and need to be put over someone's knee.'

A hot flush flooded Poppy's face as he glared at her. 'Not yours,' she murmured huskily, fighting the urge to squirm in her seat.

'You are turning out to be one of the most exasperating women I have ever met,' he muttered. 'Anyone would think I was handing you tinted marbles tied together with string.'

'That would be better. It would at least match my outfit.'

Without responding to her pithy comment, Sebastiano clamped his hand around her wrist. Before Poppy could take exception he'd propelled her to her feet and frog-marched her down the plane in front of him.

His touch sent tingles up and down her arm and she frowned. 'You have to stop doing that.'

He pushed open a door and ushered her through it. 'Doing what?'

Taking charge of her body. 'Grabbing me as if I'm yours to push around.'

'I'm not pushing you around.'

Poppy held up her hand and his came with it. 'Exhibit A, Your Honour.'

Sebastiano scowled and released her wrist. 'Exhibit B would be you being contrary. But at some point you have to get used to my touch. It might as well be before we land.'

'Get used to your touch?'

Just the thought of it sent her senses into an alarmed spin. She had an image of him stripping the clothes from her body, and then his from his own, and it wasn't a bad image.

Poppy took a step back and rubbed at her wrist, her eyes riveted to the enormous silk-covered bed that dominated the luxurious room. Before she could prevent herself, her eyes flew to his with apprehension. If he touched her now, if he kissed her as she had dreamt of him doing all week, would she have the wherewithal to deny him?

'No need to look at me like that,' he rasped. 'I meant in public. It will look a little odd if you flinch or cover me in coffee every time I get too close to you.'

Poppy took a minute to think about where her head was at, reminding herself that she was here not because he *wanted* her here, but because he *needed* her here. Which didn't mean she had to give into his every demand. Especially if she wanted to maintain her sense of self. 'Then don't get too close to me,' she said matter-of-factly.

As if he was completely exasperated with her, he shook his head. 'I brought you in here because I've organised some things for you, and you might as well sort through what you want here rather than cause a scene at the villa.'

Poppy followed his line of sight and noticed a row of glossy carrier bags with couture names stacked neatly along the wall. She frowned. 'What things?'

'Clothes. Shoes. Handbags.' He waved his hand dismissively. 'Things women need.' He frowned. 'I texted Paula on the way to the airport. She took care of it.'

Heated embarrassment filled Poppy's cheeks. So that was the reason their take-off had been delayed. He couldn't have made it any plainer that she was beneath him and she couldn't deny the ripple of hurt that passed through her. 'Really?' She strolled over to the first bag and opened it up. Could a girl feel any more inept than she did already?

Carelessly pulling the first item she touched out of one of the shiny bags, she unwrapped the tissue paper and held up an exquisite blue skirt. 'A skirt. Thanks. I never would have thought to pack one.'

'I had to guess your size,' he said, a little discomfited. 'I hope it fits.'

Poppy smiled serenely. She intended to make him feel more than discomfited by the time she finished with him.

'I'm sure Paula is exemplary at her job.' Then a horrible thought struck her. 'Oh God, you didn't tell her they were for me, did you?'

His eyes narrowed at her panic. 'No, I didn't tell her that. And actually I've never asked Paula to buy a woman clothing before so yes, I hope she did a good job.'

'Really?' Poppy put a hand to her chest. 'That makes me feel so special.' She unwrapped another, smaller parcel of tissue. This time a demi-cup bra fell out of it. *Perfect.*

She let a soft smile touch her lips as she dangled it in front of him, gratified when his eyes darkened. 'And underwear. I never would have thought to pack underwear either. It's so lucky you're around, Mr Castiglione. What would a girl do without you?'

A muscle ticked in his jaw as he registered her sarcasm.

'It's Sebastiano,' he said, frowning. 'And I take it from your tone that you don't approve?'

'Smart,' she said, dropping the offending items back in the bag and slapping her hands on her hips. 'But I packed my own clothes and shoes and *women's* things, thank you very much.'

'Damn it, Poppy.' He rubbed the back of his neck in frustration. 'Stop being so stubborn about this. That duffle bag of yours was half-empty.'

Affronted, Poppy glared at him. 'My duffle bag is none of your concern.'

A low-level growl emanated from his throat as if he had reached the end of his tether. 'Any other woman would be more than pleased with what I'm offering. No-strings-attached jewels and designer clothes. An all-expenses-paid holiday in Italy.'

'Then ask those women to Italy.'

'I don't want to ask those women to Italy!' he all but bellowed.

'Then you'll have to put up with me.' She whirled around to stalk out of the room but his hands descended on her shoulders.

'Okay, what's wrong?'

Poppy stared up at him. *The man had to ask!*

'I don't want your designer clothes,' she said, her temper and insecurities sparking in equal measure. 'And as for the holiday? I have to spend time impressing people I've never met and pretending to be in love with a man I hardly know. I don't know any woman who would want to do that.'

'Unfortunately I know plenty.'

'Like I said—invite them.'

'You know I can't.'

'So says the man who makes trillion-dollar deals every day.'

He had the grace to look contrite. 'You don't like me

very much, do you?' His voice was low and packed with an emotion she couldn't identify.

Poppy's chin came up. 'It's not that I don't like you. It's more that you're not my type.'

He looked startled for a moment. 'You're into women?'

Poppy rolled her eyes. 'It's a testament to your enormous ego that you would think the only reason I wouldn't find you attractive is because I'm gay. But I'm not. The truth is, you're entitled, and you have no sense of humour.'

A muscle ticked in his jaw again. 'I have a sense of humour. It might not extend to wearing Mickey Mouse watches, but I have one.'

Poppy gaped at him, affronted. 'What's wrong with my watch?'

'Nothing,' he said levelly. 'I just wouldn't date a woman who wore one.'

Poppy's lips pursed. 'Well, you do this weekend, because I never take it off.'

His eyes narrowed. 'It's special to you?'

'Very.'

'Did Simon give it to you?'

'Yes. As a matter of fact, he did. Do you have a problem with that?'

'Take it from me,' he said with lethal softness. 'You're selling yourself too cheap.'

Poppy made a choking sound in the back of her throat. 'I can't believe you just said that.'

'Dio!' He stalked away from her and then back, frustration vibrating through his big body. 'You know, you would try the patience of a saint.'

'I would!'

He towered over her, all six-foot-four of outraged male, and for one heart-stopping moment Poppy thought he was going to pull her into his arms and kiss her. And she wanted him to kiss her. So desperately it made her knees tremble.

'I did not mean to insult you,' he said stiffly.

Poppy's chin jerked up. 'Well, you did. But unfortunately for you, your grandfather thought you'd date someone who would wear this watch, so you'll just have to deal with it.'

His mouth flattened into a grim line. 'I doubt my grandfather made it past your dazzling smile to even notice the watch,' he growled. 'Wear the clothes, don't wear the clothes; I don't care. Just make this look real.'

He stared at her as if he had a lot more to say on the subject but thought better of it, stalking out of the room and leaving a vacuum of deflated air in his wake.

Poppy sank down onto the edge of the bed. She was stunned by the argument they had just had. She never argued. Never. Easygoing by nature, she was the kind of person who got along with everyone, both men and women. So he had bought her clothes for the weekend, so what? It wasn't as if she wanted him to like her for herself. She didn't care what he thought of her. It was unlikely that she'd ever get to work for SJC in the future anyway so...what was her problem?

Sexual frustration, a small voice said. Sexual frustration for a man who was using her, just like every other person she had ever got close to other than Maryann.

She sighed. She was going to have to get over the fact that she disliked that he was using her too and figure out how to play the game. Because she had agreed to this deal and, if he wanted some besotted girlfriend to convince his grandparents that he was a reformed rake, then that was exactly what he was damned well going to get!

CHAPTER SIX

'POPPY, THIS IS my grandmother, Evelina. Nonna, this is Poppy Connolly.'

'*Buongiorno*, Poppy, *come stai*? It is lovely to finally meet you. Giuseppe spoke so highly of you.'

Poppy beamed at the beautifully coiffed Italian woman and wound her arm through Sebastiano's, leaning against his side to give the impression of the picture-perfect girlfriend. 'It's nice to meet you too. You have a beautiful home.' Which was an understatement. The pale pink mansion that was built on a rugged bluff in the heart of the Amalfi coast, and surrounded by palatial gardens, was a place mere mortals only got to see in *Vogue Living*. Or Bond films. And she should know. Simon had made her sit through enough of those of late.

'Thank you. Now, please, you must come inside. It is a sunny day but winter still has us in its grip.'

As they made their way up the stone steps to the portico entrance, Poppy gazed up at Sebastiano adoringly. 'Thank you for bringing me, darling.'

His eyes glittered down into hers. 'My pleasure, *pumpkin*,' he murmured, his eyes conveying a warning that he was unhappy, though why that should be was beyond her. This whole charade made her nervous, and he was the one who had told her to make it look real between them.

'Come through to the living room,' Evelina bade them. 'I've organised refreshments.'

Stepping into a lavish room straight out of a bygone century, Poppy headed straight for the large picture windows that showcased the deep-blue sea and rugged coastline beyond. Magnificent candy-coloured houses perched along the hillside while sleek-hulled yachts bobbed in the harbour. 'Oh, wow,' she murmured. 'I'd heard the Italian Riviera was beautiful but this is something else.'

'Is this your first time in Italy, Poppy?'

'Yes.' She smiled at Evelina. 'It's my first time out of England.' She moved to stand beside Sebastiano and didn't have to look at him to know he was on edge. 'I was so surprised when Sebastiano invited me, wasn't I, honey?'

She smiled up at him, trying to coax an answering smile from him, but when it came it was more of a snarl. 'You certainly were.'

'Then you must make sure you show Poppy some of our wonderful country, Sebastiano. Do you take cream in your coffee, Poppy?'

'Yes, thank you.' She took the dainty cup Evelina offered and sipped at the rich brew. 'Oh, this is heavenly.' She breathed, closing her eyes to better savour the taste. 'I'd heard that Italy does the best coffee.'

'Where is Nonno?' Sebastiano barked impatiently, his eyes blazing down at her as if she was somehow responsible for his grandfather's absence.

'He is still at the office,' his grandmother murmured. 'He was delayed but said to tell you he would be back in time for dinner.'

Catching Sebastiano's irritated glance at his watch, Poppy hunted around for a distraction and found it in the form of a cluster of framed photos on the far wall. So far she was doing all the work in making their relationship look authentic and she was fast running out of ideas on how to keep it up. 'Are these family photos?' she asked, feeling Sebastiano stiffen beside her.

'*Si,*' Evelina confirmed softly. 'This is our beautiful family.'

Intrigued, Poppy strolled over to the wall. Her eyes skimmed over the twenty or so frames, stopping on one of a boy holding on to the stern of a yacht. 'Is this you as a boy?' she asked Sebastiano, smiling at the carefree look on his face as the breeze caught his dark hair, the potential of his wide shoulders already evident even though he must have been about ten in the shot.

Sebastiano stopped beside her. 'Yes,' he said curtly.

Poppy glanced at him curiously, unsure as to why he wouldn't be happy that she was looking at the photos. She glanced at the other frames that showed a very normal, happy family. For some reason she had expected that Sebastiano's family would be snobbish and distant but, seeing this wall of coveted memories, she could already tell that they were the type of family she admired the most. Close. Supportive. *Loving.* It made her heart ache for something she had always wanted but had never been able to find.

'And this?' She pointed to a photo of a young girl in a ballet costume.

'My cousin.' He leant close and she instinctively stilled. 'What are you doing?' he murmured gruffly, his hand firm on her shoulder. To his grandmother it might look like a loving gesture, but there was so much tension radiating off him Poppy knew it was the exact opposite.

'I'm looking at photos,' she murmured, risking a glance into his stormy gaze. 'Just as you did at my place. Why are you so tense all of a sudden?'

'I'm not tense.'

Before she could check herself, she ran a hand over one corded shoulder and felt the muscles bunch beneath her fingertips. Fire flitted along her nerve endings and she did her best to ignore it. 'You certainly feel tense. You just jumped six foot in the air.'

'Listen, I—'

'Sebastiano, come stai tesoro mio?'

Poppy turned to see a willowy blonde woman heading towards them, a wide smile on her face.

Embracing Sebastiano, she gave him a traditional kiss on each cheek. *'E così bello vederti.'*

'It's good to see you too,' Sebastiano murmured.

Poppy swallowed heavily, a sick feeling invading her stomach. Was she about to meet one of Sebastiano's ex-girlfriends?

'I'm sorry, I shouldn't be speaking in Italian.' The woman smiled at her warmly, her brown eyes alight with interest. 'I'm Nicolette, Sebastiano's cousin—and you must be Poppy. Welcome. You can call me Nicole, like everyone else does.'

His cousin! Poppy was disconcerted to find that she didn't have to pretend her sense of relief. She smiled in greeting and had no choice but to accept a warm kiss on each cheek as well. Unused to being welcomed into a family so wholeheartedly, she felt something inside her clench in reaction. She had always been openly affectionate with Simon, replacing the mother he'd never known from an early age, but she wasn't so used to being embraced herself.

As if sensing her unease, Sebastiano ran his hand down her arm, as if he were gentling a startled animal. The gesture of comfort was so unusual, she felt instantly overwhelmed.

'Please don't tell me Nonna invited the whole family over tonight?' he drawled to his cousin.

Nicolette laughed. 'We invited ourselves.' Then she turned to Poppy. 'Giulietta and I are dying to hear all about how you landed our elusive cousin. We think it's fantastic, by the way.'

'Oh, well, thank you. I think.' Now that she'd had a moment to take stock, Poppy couldn't help liking this woman and she gave Sebastiano an amused look. 'It wasn't easy.

What with all the supermodels he always has hanging off him.'

Nicolette laughed and Sebastiano scowled. 'Okay, I can already see you two are going to be trouble together. I think I'll take Poppy upstairs to rest before dinner.'

'Rest?' Nicolette gave him an impish wink. 'Is that what they call it nowadays, cousin?'

'Don't embarrass Sebastiano and his guest, Nicole,' Evelina scolded, her eyes shining with happiness. 'I don't want to scare him away when he has not been home in so long.'

Poppy felt Sebastiano tense again and wondered what had put that distant look in his eyes. Then he put his hand in the small of her back and she couldn't think at all.

'No fun, Nonna,' Nicole complained. 'We've been waiting for Sebastiano to fall in love for a long time. At least let me enjoy the moment.'

'Just wait till it's your turn, cousin,' Sebastiano drawled, ushering Poppy ahead of him.

'*Pah*, it's never going to happen!' Nicole lamented. 'I'm going to die an old virgin.'

'Nicolette!'

'Sorry, Nonna.' Nicole giggled, clearly not sorry at all. 'Okay, I'll be quiet now. You two run along and *rest*.'

Poppy threw Nicole a bemused smile. She'd never had a girlfriend growing up but, if she had, she would have wanted one as bubbly and lively as Nicolette.

Trailing Sebastiano up the moulded stone staircase, she was out of breath by the time he ushered her through a solid wooden door.

'*Dio,*' he muttered. 'What made me ever think this weekend was going to be easy?'

Poppy blinked up at him. 'Those long billionaire breakfasts?'

'I never said billionaire breakfasts,' he growled, dragging a hand through his hair. 'And what was with all the touching downstairs?'

'You told me to make it look real between us so I was playing my part.' Poppy glanced around the beautifully appointed sitting room and across to another set of French doors that overlooked the sea. 'I'm a pretty affectionate person so...if this was a real relationship, I'd probably touch you.' *A lot*, she silently added.

'Well, I'm not overly affectionate, so you can cut that out right now.' His eyes narrowed as they swept over her. 'Unless of course you're looking to make this real.'

Poppy frowned, hearing the edge in his voice. 'Of course I'm not looking to make this real. Why would you even think that?'

'Never mind, just...follow my lead in this.'

Poppy shrugged. 'Whatever you say, boss.' She walked over to the French windows. 'Your home is like something out of a fairy tale,' she murmured, taking in the quaint coloured houses nestled around the harbour town. 'You're so lucky to live here.'

'I don't live here any more.' He shrugged out of his jacket and tossed it on the edge of a white sofa. 'When I visit Italy, I stay in Rome.'

Poppy felt her curiosity pique at his offhand comment. 'So where do you call home?'

'I have houses in London and Boston. I spend my time where I'm needed the most.'

'Don't you get sick of packing a suitcase?' she asked, trying not to ogle his body in his fitted sweater. 'When you go from home to home.'

'I don't pack a suitcase. I have a wardrobe in each house.'

'Oh, right.' Could the gap between their two worlds be any wider? 'Me too.'

A reluctant grin flashed across his face. 'I apologise for

my cousin ambushing you before. I wasn't expecting to see my extended family until tomorrow night.'

'It's fine.' She shrugged. 'At first I thought she was an old girlfriend, but of course, what would an old girlfriend be doing here? But she was so nice it was hard not to like her. Is she always so bubbly?'

'Will you accuse me of having no sense of humour if I say "unfortunately"?'

Poppy laughed. 'Probably. But you love her anyway, right?' she asked softly.

'She's family. Of course I love her.'

A dark cloud settled over Poppy just as the wintry sun ducked behind a grey cloud, casting the lovely vista in shadows. She instinctively wrapped her arms around her torso. There was no 'of course' about it; being family did not guarantee anybody actual love.

Realising that Sebastiano was watching her with those keen, intelligent eyes, she moved away from the window. 'Nicole said that there would be others at dinner tonight. How many more of you are there?'

'Nicole's older sister, Giulietta, and her partner, Giancarlo. As well as my uncle Andrea and my aunt Elena. My uncle will most likely drink too much wine before the first course is served and fall asleep on the sofa, and my aunt will reprimand him to no end.'

'It sounds lovely.' She found herself envious of his closeness with his family. 'Is there anything else I should know?'

'Not really. We are a very small lot by Italian standards, which is one of the reasons I suspect my grandfather wants me to hurry up and settle down.'

'And holding the family business over your head to get you to do it.'

'Something like that.'

'It sounds a bit Machiavellian,' she commented.

'My grandfather doesn't mean it to be. He just has a bee in his bonnet over my single status.'

'Because you're the last Castiglione male.'

'Exactly.'

'Well, that's a relief, because he seemed really nice when I met him.' She frowned. 'But what about one of your other relatives? Can't they run the company?'

'Giulietta is in fashion, Giancarlo is a flourishing wine maker and Nicolette is in engineering. Since my uncle is an artist and my aunt a homemaker, they were never contenders.'

'So that leaves only you.'

'Yes.' His tone was curt. 'My father would have taken over but… Anyway, my grandfather means well. He just thinks I work too hard.'

'Everyone thinks you work too hard,' Poppy said lightly. 'It's admirable on one hand and a bit scary on the other. Even your social engagements are usually for work.'

'I run six miles a day. Sometimes more.'

She made a face. 'Running? Seems like more work to me. Not that I don't admire the results.'

Realising what she had just revealed, she blushed, and his eyes gleamed with interest. 'Did you just tell me you found me attractive, Poppy?'

'No.'

His smile told her he knew she was lying. 'That's a relief because I'm not your type, remember?'

'Well, you're not if we're talking boyfriend material, but as a boss you're pretty sensational.'

'So what is *boyfriend* material for you?'

'Um, I don't know.' She smoothed her hair back behind her ears. 'Someone kind and considerate. Someone with a sense of humour and who is interested in making a difference in the world.' Someone who would love her for herself and understand that she would always put her brother's needs first. 'You know, the usual suspects.'

'You didn't mention money.'

'I'd rather find someone who was trustworthy than someone with a large bank account. And anyway, I intend to make my own money so I don't have to rely on someone else for the rest of my life.'

He shook his head. 'I find that hard to believe.'

Poppy blinked at him. 'Why?'

'My experience of women is that they're all looking for a man to pay the bills. Are you telling me you're the exception to the rule?'

'Since I pay my own bills and am happy to do so, I suppose I am.'

Uncomfortable with the way he was studying her, Poppy cleared her throat. 'Maybe you should tell me where I'll be sleeping so I can get ready for dinner.'

With me, was Sebastiano's first thought.

Don't be an idiot, was his second.

He wasn't sure if this beautiful, guileless woman was for real but some deep-seated part of him wanted her to be. She'd been surprising him ever since he'd collected her from her flat, and he'd only realised when she had opened her front door how much he had been looking forward to seeing her. He had even made an excuse to visit the legal department during the week, and that impulse had irritated him so much he'd filled the rest of his week with back-to-back meetings.

He didn't know what it was about her, but she got to him. Those bold blue eyes that could spark with both humour and fire and held a wealth of secrets; that mouth that was inviting even when it was pressed into a taut line; her body... *Dio*, her bones were so delicate, her figure so slender, he'd have to go easy on her at least the first time.

The first time?

Dio!

There would be no first time between them. No matter that her sweet scent filled the space between them and made him salivate; no matter that she turned him on to the point that the women in his past became faceless names whenever she touched him. She had made it more than clear that she wasn't interested in him—that he wasn't her type. And that was for the best. Even if it grated.

What had she said on the plane? That he was *entitled*? And with *no sense of humour*? By God, when she had said that he'd had an overwhelming urge to toss her onto the bed and show her just what he did have to offer. And downstairs, when she had clung to him like a barnacle on a rock, it was all he'd been able to do to stop himself from hauling her into a dark corner and pulling her skirt up to her waist. Unused to feeling so caught up over a woman, Sebastiano scowled when he realised that he still hadn't answered her question about the sleeping arrangements.

'You'll be sleeping in my bed,' he said gruffly, irritation warring with arousal as her gorgeous eyes flew to his.

'Your bed?'

'Relax, Poppy, I won't be in it.'

'Well, I didn't expect that you would but—where will you sleep?'

Sebastiano glanced at the white sofa against the window that was designed for high tea rather than sleep.

Her eyes followed his gaze and she frowned. 'You can't sleep there. It's not long enough.'

'It will do.'

'No.' She shook her head. 'I can bunk down on the sofa. Believe me, I've had worse.'

Sebastiano frowned, remembering that she had been brought up in the foster care system. The knowledge had played on his mind all the way to Italy. 'How much worse?'

She crinkled her nose. 'Oh, you know—*worse*.' She

glanced around his luxuriously appointed room. 'Or perhaps you don't. Anyway—I'll take the sofa.'

'Actually, I do know,' he said, affronted by her belief that he was some spoilt, rich ingrate. 'I did a year in the army when I was younger, and no matter which country you're in the ground is always hard.'

'Okay, I stand corrected,' she said, waving off his irritation as if she was completely unperturbed by his scowl. 'But I'm still taking the sofa.'

A muscle ticked in Sebastiano's jaw. 'You're my guest. You get the bed.' And, so saying, he moved to the door to his old bedroom and pushed it open.

Poppy followed reluctantly and glanced inside. 'Big,' she murmured as she took in his king-sized bed, her husky tone forcing Sebastiano to grip the doorframe a little harder.

'What did you expect?' he asked, his voice deeper than usual.

She looked up at him, her blue eyes wide, and he cursed himself for his provocative question. She wasn't here for sex so best he get his mind back on track.

'Perhaps I could use a spare room,' she murmured.

Sebastiano stepped away from her and poured himself a glass of water from the pitcher standing on the sideboard. 'And how would that look to my family?'

'I don't know. I had imagined your grandparents would be old-fashioned about sex before marriage and give us separate rooms anyway.'

'I'm a grown man, *bella*. They would think it strange if I wasn't sleeping with you. And my grandparents have moved with the times. Apparently my grandmother even has a smart phone.'

Her soft mouth curved into a delightful smile. 'You sound put out.'

Sebastiano dragged a hand through his hair. 'This whole weekend has put me out.'

'Because you have to be here with me?'

'Because I have to be here at all.'

She frowned. 'I thought you loved your family.'

'I do love my family. This...' He waved his hand around and had no idea what he was doing. The last thing he wanted to do was open up to a woman he barely knew and tell her that this villa brought back too many painful memories he'd rather bury deep than think about. 'Never mind.' He took a deep, steadying breath. 'Usually we don't dress for dinner, but since the tribe has been invited you might want to make it semi-formal.'

'Thanks. Oh—and one other thing.'

Intending to plunge himself into work, Sebastiano paused with his hand on his laptop. 'What is it?' he asked curtly.

'Even though you don't seem to want to be here you might want to be a little less obvious about the whole work thing. A man in love would take some time to enjoy himself with his girlfriend while he was here.'

Sebastiano frowned. 'What are you talking about?'

'Before, when you found out your grandfather wasn't available, you kind of looked like you wanted to kick something.'

'That's because I did want to kick something.'

Her sparkling eyes disarmed him completely. 'Like I said, you might want to tone that down a little. I mean, isn't the whole purpose of me being here to show you in a new light?'

Unaccustomed to having his actions questioned, Sebastiano frowned. 'The reason you're here is to do whatever I say.' He noted the way her eyebrows hit her hairline and it only aggravated him more. 'Trust me, Poppy. I know what I'm doing.'

'Oh, right, because you—'

'Don't you dare say it,' he growled, secretly astonished at

her temerity when he realised the direction of her comment. He'd been a superior ass when he'd told her he could handle anything, because he closed billion-dollar deals every day and he didn't even think his impish cousin would tease him about it as openly as Poppy did.

She laughed softly and held her hands up in mock surrender. 'I wasn't going to.'

But they both knew that she was and something pulled tight in Sebastiano's chest when he realised that her light teasing had been to pull him out of the mood he'd been about to spiral into.

He stared at the closed bedroom door long after she had disappeared through it. Usually the women he dated thought more about themselves than anyone else, and he wasn't completely comfortable to think that Poppy wasn't one of them.

CHAPTER SEVEN

POPPY CLOSED THE door on Sebastiano's scowling face and leant back against it, waiting for the butterflies to resettle in her stomach. She didn't know why she felt the need to tease him; she just couldn't seem to help herself. He was so serious most of the time, so controlled, and she couldn't help but wonder what had made him that way, and whether he allowed anyone to penetrate beneath his aloof exterior.

Let it go, Poppy, she urged her curious side. *You're not here to fix the guy.*

Sighing, she spied the bed and the row of shopping bags that must have been delivered to her room while she had been downstairs. Right now she longed for more than a shower and a change of clothing. She longed to go home, the instinctive need to protect herself riding her hard.

She checked her phone for any further messages from Simon but he must still be in the movie. She smiled as she remembered snapping a heap of photos on her phone on the drive from Naples to the house and sending them to him. He had replied with a playfully annoyed face after he'd received them, telling her that he should be there with her.

Next time she'd love to bring him. Not that next time would be any time soon. Once Poppy finished her degree, she would be working hard to give them both a better standard of living, not holidaying in exotic locations such as this.

Glad for that reality check, she headed for the bathroom, sighing at her pale complexion. The weekend had barely started and already she felt like a fish out of water.

After washing and drying her hair with the luxurious products set out on the marble bench top, Poppy padded back into the bedroom and paused in front of a walk-in closet as big as a shipping container. Someone—most likely one of the discreet white-coated servants she had noticed earlier—must have unpacked her duffle bag because her measly amount of clothing hung in a forlorn row as if the wearer had needed to escape in a hurry and had left the dregs of their wardrobe behind.

An image of Nicole in her svelte purple dress slid into Poppy's mind. She knew she could never pull off Nicole's polished poise if she spent a century getting ready, but she guessed that whatever was in those bags beside the bed would get her closer to the mark than what was currently hanging limply in front of her.

Was she being silly in her insistence that she wasn't going to wear any of them?

Probably, and she recalled the vow she had made back on the plane to make their relationship look real. A pretence that would require a lot of acting, and well, what was an actor without a costume? Or a knight without armour? What was a person without integrity?

The thought stayed her. She was already compromising hers by fabricating this relationship with Sebastiano so that he could take control of his family's company; she wasn't going to expound that by pretending she was someone she wasn't.

It was probably only pride driving her decision to ignore the shiny bags, but it was all she had to hold her head up high, and she wouldn't compromise that.

Sighing deeply, she once again scanned her clothes and pulled a green jersey dress from the hanger. She had found it at a vintage shop and Maryann liked it on her.

'It shows off your legs,' she'd said. 'Especially when

you team it with those sexy black heels with the little strap around the ankle.'

Dressing quickly, she tied her hair back in a stylish ponytail and slid her feet into said sexy black heels. She rarely had a chance to dress up in her day-to-day life, and a fizz of excitement invaded her belly as she stared at herself in the mirror.

Would Sebastiano admire her in the dress, or would he be angry that she was not wearing one of his offerings?

Poppy's lips flattened as she realised where her thoughts were leading her.

She didn't want Sebastiano to like her or approve of her; she just needed to convince his family she was someone he could fall in love with. Her gaze fell to her Mickey Mouse watch. So far she'd never had any cause to take it off and, since it was more playful than garish, she stubbornly decided that she wasn't going to now. No matter that Sebastiano would not date a woman who wore it. As she'd said to him, he could invite someone more sophisticated to Italy if image was so important to him!

Hearing a text come in on her phone, she smiled as she opened Simon's message telling her all about the movie he had just seen. Texting back made her feel more like her usual self, and she was so absorbed she didn't even hear Sebastiano until he bit out a terse. 'Let me know when you're done.'

Whirling around, her heart skipped a beat when she saw him standing in the open doorway.

'I did knock, but you were too busy on your phone to hear it.'

Poppy took in his black trousers and matching shirt that was rolled to his elbows. He looked every inch the arrogant bad boy that he was and she warned her heart to settle down. A woman would have to be mad—or incredibly sure of herself—to take on a man like him. And she was neither.

Still, she was only human, and an unwilling awareness flared inside her, along with that old feeling of wanting to desperately hold on to something but knowing it would never be yours to keep.

'Right.' She moistened her dry lips. 'I take it it's show time?'

His eyes fell on the unopened bags by the bed and his lips tightened. 'Like I said, follow my lead and everything will be fine.'

Poppy smoothed down the skirt of her dress and walked towards him. 'What does "follow your lead" mean, exactly?'

'It means stop fretting.' He glanced at her fingers that were pleating a fold into her skirt.

'I'm not fretting,' she said, feeling uncomfortably exposed by the fact that he had picked up on her nervous habit. 'Okay, maybe I am a little, but—' A wave of panic assailed her and she grabbed on to his forearm without meaning to. 'But I really don't think—'

'This will work?'

He raised a brow and Poppy scowled.

'Well, I don't see how it can,' she said hotly, annoyed that he wasn't taking her concerns seriously. 'We're from different worlds, Sebastiano, and I feel badly about lying to your family. They're really nice and I'm not that great an actress. They've probably already seen through me.'

'So, if they were fire-breathing dragons, that would make it easier?'

She glared at him. 'I'm being serious.'

'So am I.' He sighed and raked a hand through his hair. 'To address your first concern about us being from different worlds, my *nonna* worked in my *nonno*'s kitchen when they met so, believe me, you working for me will just seem romantic to them. As to your second concern...' He shrugged. 'We won't lie.'

Poppy blinked as she absorbed his words. 'I think you might have to clarify what you mean,' she said warily. 'Your cousin already said she couldn't wait to hear the details of how I *landed* you!'

'All you need to do is pretend that we're in a relationship but as to the details…we stick to the truth as much as possible. We met six weeks ago when you came to work for me—'

'Technically we met a week ago.'

'A minor detail.' He shrugged. 'We can say we only got together recently—which is true—so our relationship is still new.'

She frowned. 'I thought you wanted me to pretend that you're the light of my life?'

Sebastiano's lip curled sardonically. 'Since seeing Nicole's unbounded enthusiasm, I think it's too difficult to pull off the whole "desperately in love" angle. It will have to be enough that my family thinks we are a couple. If my grandfather interprets that as a lifetime commitment, that's his problem, not mine.'

Poppy bit her bottom lip, expecting to feel relief at his words, but somehow feeling slightly deflated instead. Why she should, though, she didn't know. Of course a man like Sebastiano would find it difficult to pretend to be desperately in love with a woman like her. Hadn't he already said as much?

'Fine,' she managed in a falsetto voice. 'But what if that's not enough for him to hand you the CEO position?'

It was a good reminder of why they were both here and Sebastiano grabbed on to it so that he wasn't tempted to grab onto her and show her all the reasons it would be a good idea for them to forget dinner and share his very comfortable, very *big* bed behind them. 'I'll cross that bridge when I come to it.'

'Okay,' she said, grabbing a brightly coloured shawl from the back of a chair. 'It's your show.'

Sebastiano looked down at her as she came to stand beside him. It was his show, so why didn't he feel like he was running things?

Frowning, he deliberately invaded her space, fascinated by the tiny pulse point that started fluttering in her creamy throat. 'It is my show, and what I need from you is no unnecessary touching, no inquisitive questions and no elaborating on our story. Do you think you can do that, intern?'

The pulse at the base of her throat jumped before speeding up even more. 'Of course I can do that.' She gave him a smile that didn't quite reach her eyes. 'One ready-made, non-adoring, fake girlfriend to go.'

'Good.' He let out a calming breath and ignored the tightness in his chest.

Of course she couldn't do that, Sebastiano thought two hours later as frustration turned his muscles hard. The woman was a law unto herself and she didn't even seem to know it. A human wrecking ball. Not that she had spilt anything on him this time. No, she was just playing havoc with his senses: brushing up against him every time she shifted in her seat; stroking her fingers across his forearm every time she needed something. Water. Salt. Sugar. The last time she'd leant into him, he'd nearly dumped the entire contents of the table in front of her so she wouldn't have to ask for anything else.

And all the while she was completely charming, regaling his family with stories about working for his company, and how she had accidentally thrown coffee over him when they had met—leading Giulietta to ask if it had been love at first sight.

Poppy had thrown to him for that one, nibbling on her

plump lower lip as if she wasn't sure how to respond. And how was he supposed to answer, other than to say yes?

Che palle! His family would have him setting a wedding date if he wasn't careful!

She had also talked about how she wanted to help those less fortunate than she was when she finished law, and all the while she hadn't revealed any real details about her past, always managing to draw his family's interest back onto more present day issues. She was slick, he'd give her that, but little did she realise that, the less she revealed about herself, the more he wanted to know.

Who was he kidding? he thought as she murmured another apology after her leg brushed his; the only thing he wanted to know about her was how she would taste if he kissed her.

Right now she'd taste of Riesling, heat and passion. A passion he suspected she would try to deny before it even bloomed, but one he was starting to crave to draw out of her.

His hands clenched into fists at his sides. His body ached to find out if he was right, if she was as responsive as he'd imagined she would be that morning she had knotted his tie.

He warned himself to give it a rest because the more he thought about her in that way the more he wanted her. And, apart from the fact that he didn't want to lead her on, there was something about her that was dangerous to his equilibrium. Something that warned all his instincts to back away and keep going.

'Sebastiano,' she murmured beside him. 'Is everything okay?'

And that was another annoying habit she had. She seemed to be able to read him better than anyone else he knew. 'Of course, *bella*,' he said smoothly. 'Why do you ask?'

'Well…' She gave him a worried sideways look. 'You're very tense again.'

'I'm tired,' he excused. Which wasn't an actual lie; it just wasn't whole truth.

Before she could rebuke his assertion, her mobile phone started ringing. He had noticed her texting on it through-out the day, and again when she'd been waiting on him to bring her downstairs. The damned thing never seemed to be far from her side, and for some reason that annoyed him about her too.

'Excuse me,' she murmured softly, sliding her chair back. 'I have to take this.'

'Va bene, va bene,' his grandfather said indulgently, even though he was a tough old bird who banned mobile phones from his dinner table.

Scowling, Sebastiano watched a tender smile flit across Poppy's lips before she stepped outside the French doors onto the balcony that led to the pool pavilion and beach beyond.

Who was she talking to? Simon?

He had no idea who the man was but it grated that he'd overheard her tell him that she loved him when he'd arrived to collect her. It might not have mattered if she hadn't been so evasive when he'd asked about it, but she had been, piqu-ing his interest even more.

'Sebastiano?'

Was he a boyfriend? A lover? And if so what did he think of her coming to Italy with him? Did the poor sod even know?

'Sebastiano, dove hai la testa?' his grandfather asked with a soft chuckle.

Where was his head? Good question. Not where it should be. About to shove back his chair and go after Poppy, he was foiled when Nicolette did it first. 'It's cute to see you worrying about your new girlfriend,' she said, completely misinterpreting his distractedness. 'But you relax. I'll go find her and make sure she doesn't get lost.'

Foiled by yet another irritating female, Sebastiano subsided back in his chair and wondered if he would look too 'focused' if he started talking business with his grandfather...

A smiling Nicole came over to join Poppy, who noticed Sebastiano had come outside and was speaking with his grandfather. Hopefully they were finalising the business Sebastiano had come here to do so that they could leave early. It would be much better for her strained nerves if he did. Though even as she had the thought she knew there was no way Sebastiano could miss his grandparents' wedding anniversary tomorrow night.

'Gorgeous view, no?'

Poppy stared out at the twinkling lights dotted around the majestic coastline and nodded. 'Unbelievable.'

'I meant the man, not the backdrop,' Nicole teased with a soft laugh.

'Oh!' Poppy smiled, or she tried to. 'Yes to both.'

'I'm really glad you're with my cousin,' she said. 'I've never seen him look at a woman the way he looks at you.'

As far as Poppy could tell, he looked at her as if he wanted to strangle her most of the time, especially when she had inadvertently cornered him into saying that he loved her. Which hadn't been entirely her fault. His terse instructions upstairs, and her worry over making their relationship look normal when she really had no idea what a normal relationship looked like, had made her fidgety. It hadn't helped that he'd sat so close to her at dinner she'd felt the press of his powerful thigh against hers every time he moved. The man just took up too much space!

'I'm sure your cousin has looked at many women the way he looks at me,' Poppy commented, wanting to down play the lie she didn't enjoy telling. She'd heard so many lies in her life so far, she'd vowed to not tell any herself, and here she was pretending to be involved with this lovely woman's cousin.

'Not that I've seen,' Nicole said. 'In fact, he's never brought a woman home to meet *la famiglia* before. It means you're important.'

Poppy frowned. 'No one?'

'No,' Nicole confirmed. 'That's how we know you're the real deal. Apart from the fact that he looks at you as if he wants to gobble you up whole.'

Poppy felt her whole face flush and Nicole was immediately contrite. '*Mi dispiace*. I'm sorry, Poppy. I didn't mean to embarrass you. It's just that I'm jealous.' She gave a dramatic sigh. 'I want a man to look at me like that one day.'

'Like what?' Sebastiano asked as he came to stand beside Poppy.

Poppy's heart kicked up at the sound of his voice, her body going on high alert. He was so close she could feel the heat of him driving out the chill of the night air.

'Like he wants to eat me up,' Nicole said.

Poppy groaned; the only thing she wanted eating her up right now was the ground.

'You're too young.' Sebastiano was deadpan. 'If any man looked at you that way, he'd have me to contend with.'

'*Pah!* I am twenty-four,' Nicole retorted hotly. 'One year younger than Poppy!'

'Like I said,' Sebastiano smiled down at her. 'Too young.'

Nicole pulled a face and Sebastiano tweaked her nose as if she were ten years old. It reminded Poppy of how she liked to fool around with Simon, and a sense of warmth invaded her heart. Initially she had thought Sebastiano just a corporate shark with no feelings but seeing his more playful side come out with his family made him more human than she would like him to be. It made him more of a man she could grow to like if she wasn't careful.

'Be warned, Poppy,' Nicolette advised her loftily. 'The Castiglione men think they own the world sometimes.'

Sebastiano laughed as his cousin wandered back inside.

'Don't listen to her,' he said, looking down at Poppy. 'We Castiglione men *know* that we own the world.'

Poppy couldn't contain a grin and shook her head. 'You are so full of yourself.'

'*Si.*'

His smile took her breath away and she shivered. He wasn't even trying to be charming and yet he was. What would happen if he actually tried to win her over?

'Are you cold?'

'No... I mean, yes. A little, but...' She paused as he draped his jacket over her shoulders. His clean scent and warmth instantly enveloped her and she breathed in deeply, warning herself to put some distance between them because she was already feeling overwhelmed by him. 'I'm sorry about earlier,' she murmured. 'That whole "love at first sight" thing at the dinner table. I didn't mean to trap you like that.'

'Didn't you?'

'Of course not.' His suspicion was as thick as a pea-souper and, frankly, insulting. 'You really have mixed with the wrong women, haven't you?'

'So my grandfather would have me believe.'

'Look, Sebastiano, I'm not likely to forget that this whole thing is phony and I'm under no illusions as to why I'm here. The problem is, I'm not used to being the centre of attention, and I don't like it.'

'What are you used to?'

His unexpected question caught her off-guard and dashed her indignation. 'What do you mean?'

'I mean, what do you do with yourself when you're not studying or working as my intern?'

Poppy shrugged. 'I work, like anyone else.' And she

ran around after her brother during those brief moments she had off.

'Work where?'

'I clean offices during the night.'

His eyes narrowed. 'During the night? Why?'

Uncomfortable to be talking about herself, Poppy made to shrug out of his jacket. 'Look, you're cold now, so—'

Sebastiano grabbed the lapels and kept the jacket in place. 'I'm not cold. Why do you clean offices at night?'

She gave a short laugh. 'For the love of it. Why do you think?'

'Okay, I deserve that,' he acknowledged impatiently. 'But why night in particular? Is it to fit in around your lecture times?'

'No, it's to fit in around my brother. I like to be there when he gets home from school.'

'I assumed your brother was still in the foster-care system.'

'No way.' She shuddered. 'I would never leave him in foster care when I'm perfectly capable of taking care of him myself.' *Well, she was now.*

She didn't like the way Sebastiano was studying her and made to put some distance between them.

Frustrated, Sebastiano gripped the lapels of her jacket more firmly, and didn't realise he had drawn her closer until her sweet scent caught on his senses, making him burn.

For some reason the idea of Poppy working hard and lugging heavy cleaning equipment around during the night while he slept bothered him immensely.

Previously he had always been coolly indifferent to a woman's needs outside of the bedroom, not wanting to encourage them to think he wanted anything more from them than the physical. Previously, until Poppy.

He scowled. He couldn't even put his interest down to the fact that he had made her off limits, because he'd felt the pull of her right from the start. No, this wasn't about his ego, it was about heat and desire and, while he might not be able to explain this compulsion to have her, he knew the only way to get rid of it *was* to have her. Have her naked, spread out and on fire for him, as he was for her. And he damned well knew she wanted him too. He'd seen the way she'd stared at his naked torso last Sunday morning, and felt the way she stiffened with awareness whenever he got too close.

Not her type?

He was more her type than whomever that Simon was who had given her the Mickey Mouse watch she treasured so dearly.

'Who's Simon?' he asked curtly. The man had been a burr in his side since he'd heard her tell him she loved him and it had become imperative that he find out more about him. So much easier to shoot an adversary down in flames when you knew who you were firing at.

Adversary?

He was getting in way over his head and he knew it.

Poppy blinked up at him. 'Simon?'

'*Si,*' he said gruffly. 'The one who gave you the watch. You were on the phone to him when I arrived at your apartment, and every time his name flashes on your damned phone you jump to respond, as if it's a fire you need to put out.'

Poppy frowned. 'You seem surprised by that.'

'I have to confess that I am.'

'I don't know why. You're obviously close to your own family. Would you not respond to a text if Nicole or Giulietta sent one?'

'We're talking about Simon, not my damned cousins.'

'I know that, but I don't see the difference.'

Sebastiano stared into her luminous blue eyes, made even bluer by the reflected light glowing from the infinity pool nearby. Something in her guileless gaze finally registered in his usually agile brain. 'Right,' he said, feeling like a fool. 'Simon is your brother.'

'Yes. Who did you...? Oh!' She clapped her hand over her mouth as if to stifle a laugh. 'You thought he was...?' She shook her head. 'Who? My lover?'

At his silence her grin widened and that only made him scowl harder. 'Of course I thought he was your lover. You told him you loved him.'

Her glee was evident in her mischievously sparkling eyes. 'Is that why you glower at me every time I use my phone?'

'You need to stop laughing.'

'You have to admit, it's kind of funny,' she said, making a meagre attempt to stifle her mirth.

Sebastiano drew her even closer, releasing the lapels of his jacket to slide his hands into the wisps of hair either side of her face. She stopped laughing instantly then, her eyes suddenly as wide as saucers. Her hair felt like silk against his fingers, her skin even softer. His eyes drifted from her mouth to the tiny pulse point flickering in the base of her throat, a sense of victory he couldn't explain coursing through him. 'Kind of funny, you think?'

'Sebastiano?' Her voice was soft and her hands came up to grip his thick wrists. 'What are you doing?'

'I'm going to give you a lesson in what *I* would do if this relationship was real.'

Only it's one-hundred-percent fake, he reminded himself right before he bent to her and covered her mouth with his. Her petal-soft lips parted on a gasp of surprise, her body stiffening beneath his touch.

Sebastiano gathered her closer, feeling her rigidity give way to a trembling need as old as time.

He groaned, pressing his lips harder over hers, seeking access to the warm recesses of her mouth. 'Open for me,

Poppy,' he growled. 'Kiss me as I've imagined you doing this past week. Let me taste you, *bella*. Let me—' Another groan escaped his lips as she did as he requested, willingly parting her mouth for him, a tiny whimper escaping her lips as his tongue swept inside.

He tilted her head back further, seeking even deeper contact with her, one hand leaving her face to skim down her body and curve around her waist, bringing her into firmer contact with his hardness. His other hand fisted her sleek ponytail, holding her steady beneath the onslaught of his hunger.

Dio, but she tasted sweet. Tasted sweet and felt sweeter. He wasn't sure he'd ever experienced a kiss like it, her hot, unguarded response making his body throb heavily.

Mine, a voice in his head chanted. *Take her*.

Some part of him questioned the desperate yearning behind that notion, but she was like a living flame in his arms, driving out rational thought, her hands gripping his shoulders, her tongue curling around his in a delicious imitation of what his was doing to hers. Hot need poured through him. He'd never experienced hunger like it and he wanted to drive her back against the nearest hard surface and take everything she had to offer.

A spear of blue fire flamed through him as she rubbed against him and he raised a hand to cup her breast, dragging his thumb across her distended nipple.

She gave a soft whimper and wrenched her mouth from his, her hands braced against his chest.

'Poppy...' He groaned, dragging her mouth back to his.

'Sebastiano, wait!'

Her cry of panic infiltrated his sluggish brain and he stilled, suddenly aware that they were standing by the pool at his family home in full view of anyone who might be watching.

Dio!

He eased his arms from around her, insanely gratified to find that she wasn't any more composed than he was.

She gazed up at him, her blue eyes blank with unsated lust. Her tongue snuck out to touch her reddened lips, and he saw the moment she came back into herself.

'Oh, God. I... We... Was somebody watching us?'

He had no idea. Really, the Pope could have been performing a holy communion and he wouldn't have noticed. 'It's possible.'

'It's possible?' Her hand went to her hair, smoothing the strands he had just dislodged, her breathing as hard as his. She stepped back, grabbing at his jacket before it slipped from her shoulders. 'Then why did you kiss me like that?'

He had no idea. 'Insurance,' he clipped out. 'If one of my family members *were* watching us, they would have no doubt that we're the real deal now.'

'Wow.' She blinked up at him. 'You're totally ruthless.'

Sebastiano took a deep breath. He couldn't remember the last time he had kissed a woman with so little self-control. And self-control was something he prided himself on. 'Not so ruthless,' he growled. 'If I was completely ruthless, I'd already have you upstairs. Naked.'

CHAPTER EIGHT

'IF I WAS completely ruthless, I'd already have you upstairs. Naked.'

Poppy's heart thudded inside her chest as those growly words once more replayed inside her head. She rolled over for the hundredth time and punched her pillow into a new shape, hoping that might help propel her towards sleep. Five minutes later, she gave up and again listened for signs that Sebastiano was having similar trouble sleeping.

Of course there was nothing but silence coming from the other room. And why would he have trouble sleeping? He probably kissed women like that for breakfast, while she—she truly understood for the first time how a woman could become stupid over a man. Something she had arrogantly assumed would never happen to her. Well, it just had. And her insides still felt quivery at the memory.

What she would like to know was how this had happened. Sure, he was sensationally good-looking and loved his family, but he was the ultimate megalomaniac bad boy who treated women poorly and whom she shouldn't feel anything for.

But she did feel something. She felt…she felt… God, she didn't know how she felt other than completely shaken by the memory of that powerful kiss. She shivered as she mentally replayed the scene moment by moment—the feel of his fingers in her hair, his tongue filling her mouth, his hand on her breast! Her own hand rose to her still sensitive flesh and she pressed her fingers against herself as he had done.

Stop! she ordered herself sharply; reliving something that shouldn't have happened in the first place wasn't going to get her to sleep any quicker. But her brain wouldn't listen. Which was just annoying. Poppy might have an inherently sunny disposition but she had always been a sensible person, even as a child. Her own mother had lamented that side of her nature and none of her foster families had liked it any better. But it had worked for her. It allowed her to compartmentalise the things that happened in her life, and it allowed her to pick herself up and move on when bad things happened.

Not that kissing Sebastiano had been bad. Quite the contrary. It had been heavenly. Earth-shattering... Poppy punched her pillow again. The truth was she had never kissed a man like that in her life. Had never felt the inclination before; too aware of her mother's under-age pregnancy and the devastation it had caused. But for those brief, wild moments in Sebastiano's arms she would have happily thrown all her cautious principles to the wind. She would have happily slaked the wild hunger he had induced in her and that still made her knees feel weak without any thought to her heart, or to Simon's welfare.

Which was completely incomprehensible and was an indication of how tired she was, and how much pretending to be his girlfriend this weekend had stressed her. In her desire not to fall at the role she was playing and displease him, she'd thrown herself into the part a little too enthusiastically. That surely helped explain her absolute abandon when he'd kissed her?

Didn't it?

Sighing heavily she closed her eyes against the faint night shadows. The thing to do was to banish the incident from her mind and make sure they were never in a position where it was likely to happen again.

* * *

For the first time in fifteen years Sebastiano woke up on the anniversary of his parents' deaths and they weren't the first thing on his mind.

Poppy Connolly was.

He didn't know whether to be pleased about that or put out.

What he did know was that somewhere between two and four am he had reached a decision to treat Poppy as if she was still one of his employees. Sebastiano never mixed business with pleasure and if he thought of her in a professional capacity he was unlikely to be tempted to kiss her again.

And pigs might fly. Backwards.

Ignoring the mocking voice in his head, he pushed to a sitting position and stretched the stiffness out of his neck. He'd lied to Poppy the day before when he'd said he'd slept on worse than this sofa. Nothing could be worse than this sofa.

Hearing that Poppy was already up and in the shower, Sebastiano beat back the urge to join her and grabbed his running shorts.

Work was usually his go-to panacea when this day dawned. Work and Scotch. Unfortunately Poppy would no doubt interrupt his work, and his grandparents would frown if he downed a bottle of Scotch before breakfast. So exercise it was.

Taking the back stairs to avoid any nosy family members he set off, grimly setting himself a challenging pace along the narrow, winding path that ran along the outskirts of the harbour village and wove in and around ancient vineyards until his lungs were heaving. It was fifteen years since he had been home at this time of the year. After today he'd make it another fifteen and send his grandparents an enormous anniversary present as compensation.

Grimacing at a twinge in his calf, he pushed himself harder, hoping that physical exertion would keep the demons at bay just as easily as alcohol.

Sex would, his unhelpful brain informed him.

Yeah, well, sex wasn't on the cards. Erotic dreams about plucky interns notwithstanding.

Another grimace shot across his face. He hadn't had a dream about a woman he couldn't have since he was a teenager. The image of Poppy coming over the top of him in a pale pink slip that slithered over her ripe breasts, her hair unbound and falling around her face as she lowered herself over him and took him deep, was now front and centre in his mind.

'Damn!' He stumbled as his foot twisted on a pebble, but at least it had jerked him out of his X-rated fantasy. Turning back, he pushed himself even harder until he came to a halt at the edge of the terraced gardens that skirted the villa. Pausing, he stretched out his calf. He had to stop thinking about Poppy. He hadn't brought her here this weekend to have sex with her. He'd brought her here to convince his grandfather that he was a changed man who deserved to take over the family company.

Deserved?

If anyone deserved it less, it was Sebastiano but, as Poppy had made him realise, he was the only one who could take over, and his grandfather needed to retire. He'd have been retired already if Sebastiano hadn't taken his eldest son from him: Sebastiano's own father.

He clenched his jaw as anger and self-loathing twisted like a tight, bitter knot inside him, threatening to pull him under. He'd been a snivelling little brat the night of the accident that had led to his parents' deaths, and he'd never let himself forget it.

Maledizione.

What had made him think that it would be okay to be

back here? On this day? He'd mistakenly thought it would prove that he had put the guilt of his past behind him, but it had only proved the opposite. He just thanked God that there were no photos of him and his parents on his *nonna*'s photo wall. Was that for his benefit, or for theirs?

He shook the sweat from his eyes and forced himself to sprint up the last steep incline towards the villa. But still the memories of that fateful day intruded into his consciousness like a jackhammer smashing through a slab of concrete.

In the days after his parents' accident when none of it had seemed real he'd walked along these hilltops until he was falling over with exhaustion, his grandparents' old Retriever keeping him company and licking away the tears he'd been unable to suppress. He'd unburdened himself on that poor old dog and a month later she too had died. No doubt from all the misery he had heaped on her. It was the only time he had let himself wallow.

Since then he'd kept to himself, working for his grandfather and branching out on his own, growing SJC into a global concern. It was something to be proud of, and he was. The company employed thousands of people around the world, but still something nagged at him. Some hollow sensation he knew would only be satisfied when he took control of CE.

Firmly resolved to focus only on his end goal, and not what sex with Poppy Connolly would be like, Sebastiano rounded the corner of the villa and spotted his grandparents, Nicolette and Poppy breakfasting on the sheltered outdoor terrace. They didn't notice him at first, their eyes focused on a gift his grandmother was unwrapping. Poppy tucked a strand of ash-brown hair behind her ear and bit into her bottom lip, and immediately the painful memories that had assailed him on his run were replaced with a much more pleasurable sort. The feel of her lips against his. Her breast in his hand.

He immediately wanted to drag her upstairs, strip the bulky sweater and jeans from her body and turn his midnight fantasies into reality.

Dio mio, *Castiglione, did that run sort nothing out in your head?*

'Bastian? Come join us,' his grandfather said, finally noticing him. 'Poppy has just given us a beautiful gift for our anniversary.'

Sebastiano's gut clenched. She had brought his grandparents a gift?

'It's exquisite,' Nicolette said. 'Who's the designer?'

A becoming flush highlighted Poppy's cheeks. Sebastiano glanced at the delicate glass-blown figurine his grandmother was carefully inspecting. It was of a horse with wings—at once whimsical and evocative. 'It's not from any particular design house; Simon did it.'

'Your brother? He's so talented,' Nicolette gushed.

'That's nice of you to say,' Poppy commented. 'I think he is too, but it's just a hobby at this stage. I took him to a glass works exhibition at the Tate Modern last year and he's become obsessed.'

Casting a cursory glance at the piece his family was admiring, Sebastiano stepped closer to Poppy. Immediately her eyes cut to his, a blush staining her cheeks. She went still and all his senses homed in on her. He'd bet that she was remembering their explosive connection the night before and he wasn't traditionally a betting man. *'Buongiorno, Poppy,'* he said, barely stopping himself from reaching for her to find out. 'You're up early.'

'I… I couldn't sleep,' she admitted, then, realising that they had a rapt audience, added, 'After you left.'

He lightly gripped the nape of her neck beneath the fall of her hair and felt her body quiver. A swift, answering response made his throb. 'I didn't want to disturb you,' he murmured as if he really had just left her bed.

'The coffee has just been poured,' his grandmother pointed out. 'Let me get you a cup.'

'That's fine, Nonna.' Sebastiano stayed her. 'I have to take a shower before I sweat all over Poppy. Nonno, what time do you want to meet today?'

'Ah, already your head is in business. This is why you are so successful, *nipote mio*, but also why you need Poppy by your side. You risk becoming less human.'

'I'm human,' Sebastiano ground out. Right now he was having a very human reaction to the woman seated so serenely at his family's breakfast table.

'Speaking of plans for the day, Bastian,' Nicolette said, 'I've asked Poppy if she'd like to come sailing on *Destino*. I thought it would be nice to show her some of the Riviera since you're going to be in meetings all day. And she's never been on a boat before. It will be her first time.'

Somehow the words *first time* stirred something in his Italian blood and, remembering Poppy's words from the day before about how 'focused' he was, Sebastiano found himself announcing that it was a great idea but that he would take her himself.

Poppy immediately objected, saying that she understood he was here to work and not entertain her. She sounded sincere but Sebastiano heard a note of panic in her voice and guessed that her reticence had more to do with last night's kiss than any altruistic concerns for his business goals. Certainly she had barely looked at him since he'd arrived on the terrace, and he didn't like it.

'Va bene, va bene,' his grandfather chimed in. 'Why do not we all go? We don't need an office to talk business and the house is about to be overrun with preparations for the party tonight.'

Unable to fault his grandfather's logic, especially with his grandmother's murmured approval, Sebastiano nearly groaned out loud. First he'd made a suggestion he hadn't meant to make, and now he and Poppy would be under scrutiny the whole time. Not that they wouldn't have been anyway with Nicolette present, but his grandparents were far more astute than his bubbly cousin.

'Terrific,' he said, grabbing a pastry from the breadbasket. 'Let me take a shower.'

'Sebastiano?'

Poppy had made her excuses at the table and rushed after Sebastiano, catching him halfway up the stairs.

His gaze swept over her as he turned and waited for her to reach him, making her agonisingly aware of her body in a way only he managed to do.

'What is it, *bella*?'

Flustered by the time she reached him, Poppy took a deep breath to steady her heart rate. 'I just wanted to say that if you would prefer to stay here and work then please do. I have some studying to get done for an exam I have in a couple of weeks anyway.'

'It's too late now,' he said unhelpfully. 'But by all means, bring your study notes if you want. And a jacket. The sun is out, but it will be cold on the water.'

'I don't expect you to babysit me, Sebastiano.'

Liking the sound of his name on her proper English tongue a little too much, Sebastiano scowled. 'I'm not babysitting you. I'm taking your advice and showing my grandfather my reformed ways. I would have thought you would be commending me rather than reprimanding me.'

Poppy might have commended him if she wasn't feeling so out of sorts. Something had changed when he had kissed her last night. She hadn't wanted to admit it but now it was all she could think about and she didn't know how to stop it.

'Why don't we just go and enjoy ourselves?' he suggested. 'If nothing else it will be a good distraction from the realities of life.'

* * *

Poppy had no time to ponder that esoteric comment until later. It came back to her as she watched Sebastiano, his legs braced wide as he steered the sleekly hulled vessel through wind-ruffled waves. Poppy pulled her jacket more firmly around her and turned her face up to the sun, the yacht's billowing white sails catching the wind as they raced across the water. She had to admit the whole experience of skimming over the clear blue sea in a shiny yacht and taking in the romantic Italian coastline was nothing short of exhilarating: the smell of the sea and the call of seagulls flying over head, the feel of the salt water spray intermittently carried on the wind as the waves crashed against the side of the boat. It was almost as exhilarating as the thrill she got from watching the man at the helm.

Sebastiano had taken over from the captain after lunch and she could tell he loved being out on the water. It was the most relaxed she had seen him since they had arrived, and again she wondered at his cryptic comment about wanting to be distracted from the realities of life.

As far as Poppy could see Sebastiano had a pretty good one, born to a privileged family who loved him dearly, and having amassed enough money to last him several lifetimes without having to think about it. Looking at him now, he was like a modern-day pirate, commanding everything and everyone around him with the authority of a man born to power, his thick sweater moulding to his broad shoulders, his glossy black hair blowing in the wind. She couldn't imagine what was missing from his life. Other than his grandfather's endorsement for him to take over as CEO, but any fool could see that that was imminent. Especially if she played her part well.

'Poppy, can you take this to Bastian?'

She glanced behind her to see Evelina holding up two steaming mugs of coffee.

'Of course.'

Rising to her feet, she made her way towards the helm, her ponytail whipping around her in the breeze. Just before she got to him his eyes gleamed with interest. 'You planning to hand that to me, or throw it at me?'

'That depends on whether you plan to keep reminding me of my faux pas every time I bring you coffee,' she countered, warning herself to keep her emotional walls in place when he showed his more playful side.

'Since it's too cold to lose my shirt, I'll not mention it again,' he promised, a slight smile tugging at his lips as he took the mug from her. 'How are you enjoying your first boating experience?'

'It's fantastic. Thank you. You've given me so many firsts I can hardly keep track.' First ride on a plane—private or commercial—first trip to Italy, first truly passionate kiss. Blushing at the direction of her thoughts, and worried he could read exactly what she was thinking, she sipped her own coffee. 'How did your meeting with your grandfather go earlier?'

'So so.' He grimaced. 'The old goat is still stalling.'

'Why would he be stalling?' Poppy asked, instantly worried. 'Do you think he doesn't believe we're a couple?'

'No, it's not that. I think he doesn't want to give up control of CE. He's as stubborn as an ox and wants everything to go his way.'

Poppy couldn't help the small smile that touched her lips, and of course he noticed.

'I do not have to have everything my way,' he denied with an arrogant tilt to his head, his eyes narrowing menacingly.

Poppy laughed softly. 'If it helps, you're usually right. Or so everyone in your office thinks.'

His eyebrow rose with cynical amusement. 'Tell my grandfather that. He might listen if it comes from you.'

He gave a frustrated sigh. 'His problem is that he doesn't trust the latest innovations, and thinks I'm going to continue current trends and off-shore our workforce.'

'It is a valid concern in this shifting employment market,' Poppy said. 'So many companies are doing it and it means less jobs now and in the future. Labour forces around the world are going to suffer.'

'I know. But I have no intention of offloading our loyal employees like yesterday's garbage. There are other measures that can be taken to lower operational costs and I intend to implement those first.'

'Give your grandfather time. I'm sure it's not easy for him to think about retiring after so many years in charge. But I'm sure you'll do right by everyone.'

'You are?'

'Don't look so surprised,' she said. 'You've done right by me so far.' Which was a surprise in itself, given her earlier experiences of human nature. 'You're a good person. I wasn't so sure of it at first.'

'I would never have guessed,' he said dryly.

Poppy chuckled. 'It's not totally my fault. You weren't very approachable that first morning, and then you were extremely pushy.' She glanced at him over the top of her mug. 'I also thought you wanted to take over your family business to increase your net worth, but I was wrong to judge you when I didn't really know you.'

'Don't make me out to be more than I am, Poppy,' he said gruffly. 'I'm nobody's hero.'

Poppy tilted her head, smoothing down her ponytail as it caught in the wind again. 'Are you afraid I'll fall for you?' She smiled easily, but the pulse in her throat had picked up speed and she was very much afraid Sebastiano had noticed it. 'I promise you, I won't. I'm innately sensible, and besides...' She glanced out to sea. 'I'm not looking for love either.'

'Why not?' Sebastiano spun the wheel and deftly ma-
noeuvred the yacht towards the family's private jetty.

Poppy shrugged. 'I have Simon to take care of and he's at
that difficult teenager stage where he needs someone solid
in his life to show him the way. I've seen what happens to
kids without direction and I don't want that to happen to
him. On top of that, I really don't have time. Between work,
Simon and study, I'm done in most days.'

'A man could help ease your load.'

'He could also add to it.' She shuddered. 'I've worked
out how to get by on my own and I like it.' She looked at
him a little self-consciously. 'Boy, conversations with you
get personal quickly.' She stepped away from him lightly.
'What time are we heading back to London tomorrow? I
have to let Simon and Maryann know.'

As the yacht docked, two burly men moved forward to
secure the ropes Sebastiano threw to them.

'I'll tell my grandparents we'll have to leave mid-morn-
ing, if that suits you.'

'Yes. Thanks.'

A small bubble inside her burst at his easy acceptance
of the end to their weekend and she told herself not to be
silly. Only naïve women fell for men like Sebastiano Castiglione and she'd let go of naïve a long time ago.

Coming above board, Giuseppe waited to help Nicolette
and Evelina down the gangplank. Without asking, Sebastiano held out his hand to Poppy. Before letting her go to
follow the others up the stone pathway, he turned her towards him.

Wondering if he was going to kiss her, she didn't realise
she had held her breath until he started talking.

'I wanted to thank you for giving my grandparents a
gift.'

'Oh.' She touched her hair self-consciously. 'That's okay.
It was very small, and it is their anniversary.'

'It meant a lot.'

'Okay, well…' Too aware of her hand still caught in his, Poppy tried to tug it free.

'One more thing.' He held her firm. 'At the risk of putting you off-side again, I asked Giulietta to organise something for you to wear tonight. And, before you refuse and tell me you don't need anything, it didn't cost me a thing.'

Poppy could see that he was expecting her to argue, but truthfully she had already worn the only dress that might have been remotely appropriate to dinner last night. Refusing another of his offerings because of pride would just be petulant. 'Thank you,' she murmured, smiling widely at the bemused expression on his face.

He blinked down at her. 'Any time, intern.'

CHAPTER NINE

POPPY STARED AT her reflection in the mirror. She was wearing a flowing halter-neck silver gown with matching stilettos that made her feel like a movie star.

She had found the gown hanging in the closet when she'd returned upstairs and even if she hadn't already agreed there was not enough pride in the world to stop her from wearing it.

Taking a deep breath, she walked through to Sebastiano's private sitting room. 'Didn't cost a thing, hey?' she chided gently, trying to offset her nerves.

Sebastiano turned, his phone to his ear, and Poppy forgot to breathe. She had never seen a man wearing a tuxedo in real life before and she doubted she'd ever see one who looked this good ever again.

Good?

Try amazing. Sexy. Powerful. *Edible*. Once again a nagging longing rose up inside her that only seemed to stir to life when he was around. She swallowed heavily.

Mr Powerful, I'm-In-Control, Multi-Billionaire Castiglione, meet Miss Average, Not-So-In-Control, Poppy Connolly.

He gave her one of his slow grins. 'It was worth every penny. You look ravishing.'

'Oh!' She swiped moist hands down over her middle, her brow arching as she fought to contain the thrill his compliment had given her. 'You lied to me!'

'Yes,' he said, completely unapologetic. He advanced towards her and heat bloomed beneath the surface of her skin at the look of intent on his face. Surely he wasn't going to…going to…?

'Turn around.'

Turn around? Dumbly, she glanced down to see that he was holding the blue velvet box she had handed back to him on the plane. His lips twisted sardonically as she stood unmoving. Then he gave her a gesture to turn to face the mirror hanging over the mantle, and unbelievably she did, her hands going to the deep vee between her breasts as he placed the exquisite pearl and diamond necklace around her neck.

What would it be like to sleep with a man like him for one night? she thought in a moment of helpless longing.

Dangerous, her sensible side returned, giving her backbone a much-needed boost of common sense.

'Like it or not, you're going to wear this for me tonight. If we were in a normal relationship I would insist on it.'

Poppy watched as he fastened the clasp at her nape, a shiver chasing itself down her spine. If they were in a normal relationship she would want to wear it for him.

Ignoring that thought, she noted that despite her being in high heels he was still so much taller than she was, so much broader. She was unable to take her eyes from him; their gazes collided and held when he looked up. Green on blue. Blue on green.

Suddenly it was difficult to breathe and Poppy was gripped by a ferocious shock of sexual arousal so powerful she couldn't move. She didn't want to move. Instead she wanted to lean back into him and rub her check along his freshly shaven jaw. She wanted to turn her head, find his mouth and have him kiss her as he had done the night before.

A throbbing awareness rose up between them and Poppy was shaken to realise that his gaze was full of the same heat and fire she imagined was in hers. Everything inside her urged her to turn in his arms, place her hands around his neck and bury her fingers in his short, dark hair before pulling his mouth down to hers.

His words from the previous night came back to her once more.

'If I was completely ruthless, I'd already have you upstairs. Naked.'

The tenor of the air thickened between them as if he too was remembering the same thing. Poppy couldn't move to save herself and Sebastiano seemed equally as riveted as his searing gaze drifted down to where the pearl nestled between her breasts.

'Sebastiano...'

His nostrils flared at her soft tone and, just when she thought he might reach for her, was desperate for him to reach for her, he stepped back.

'We should go down before my grandparents send up a search party.'

'Of course.' He didn't want her. Not like that. *Fool!*

She took a moment to smooth her hair back from her face. She had coiled it into what she had hoped was a sophisticated style, but now she felt awkward. Gauche.

'Poppy—'

'Yes, yes.' She pinned a smile on her face and prevented any further comment by placing her hand in the crook of his arm, and propelling him from the room. She suspected he knew exactly what had gone through her mind and she didn't want him to make some lame overture to make her feel better.

When they stopped at the top of the staircase Poppy threw him an enquiring glance. Tension radiated from him like a testosterone-driven force; a dark expression turning his features hard.

The murmur of voices and the clinking of glassware reached them, drawing her attention. Poppy felt her heart seize as a group of beautifully dressed guests entered the foyer, a white-coated servant draping jackets across his arm that most likely cost more than her yearly rent.

'Why have we stopped?' she asked. 'Is everything okay?'

His tanned throat convulsed as he swallowed. 'Why wouldn't it be?'

'I don't know—but you're frowning. This is a really big deal, isn't it?'

'It is.'

'Is that what's bothering you? You don't like parties? Because if you don't I'd be happy to rent a movie on my laptop and eat popcorn.'

He shook his head, a reluctant smile starting at the edge of his mouth. 'And what movie would you choose?'

'I don't know.' She hunted around in her brain for one of her all-time favourites. '*His Girl Friday*?'

'Never heard of it.'

'I'm not surprised,' she said. 'They don't show it often in Business School for Beginners.'

His eyes narrowed on her face, a curious light in his eyes. 'What is your story, Poppy Connolly?'

'My story?' She almost laughed. 'I'm probably the most boring person you'll ever come across.'

'Actually, you're one of the most fascinating. Do you really not know that?'

'Now you're embarrassing me,' she said softly. He couldn't possibly mean that, not after the way he had rejected her upstairs.

'I do mean it.'

She gave a soft laugh. 'You read minds now?'

'Your face is very expressive. It's like you wear your heart on your sleeve.'

'It's my worst trait.' She sighed. 'Whereas your worst trait is that you aren't expressive enough.'

'Still, you manage to read me. How is that?'

'I'm just observant, I guess. It comes from years of not fitting in.' She smiled uneasily at having revealed something so personal about herself, forcing a lightness into her voice. 'Am I going to be confronted tonight by an old girlfriend who will try and scratch my eyes out? Is that what's bothering you?'

Sebastiano shook his head. 'No. You will eat delicate canapés, sip the finest champagne and have a wonderful time.'

But what about you? she wanted to ask. If she didn't know better, she would say he was dreading his grandparents' party. 'That's a relief.' She gave him another bright smile. 'But, just so you know, I get fidgety when I'm nervous so I'll apologise now if I embarrass you in some way.'

He glanced down at where her fingers were pleating the fabric of his jacket. 'I had noticed that, yes.'

'Oh, sorry,' she muttered. 'Maybe you should pinch me so I know this isn't real.'

His eyebrow quirked. 'Isn't it supposed to be for the opposite reason? So you know something is real.'

'No. This already feels too real for my liking. I need a hard reality check. Your family makes me feel like I fit in.'

'You do fit in.'

'Yeah, like a ballerina at a bullfight.'

Sebastiano threw his head back and laughed. 'Look at me, Poppy.' He sobered and reached out to tilt her chin up so that her eyes met his, a frisson of awareness darting between them. 'You can fit in anywhere.'

Her heart bumped inside her chest. 'That's not true.' She had tried many times before and never fit in. 'And you know it.'

'I know some people are callous snobs, but only you can let them reduce who you are.'

'So says the man who grew up with a silver spoon in his mouth.'

'But you are wearing the silver dress, *bella*.' His smile was disarming, his eyes steady on hers. 'You're smart and beautiful, Poppy. You probably didn't hear that enough growing up, but you can take my word for it. My HR department don't hire duds.'

She let out a shaky breath; she hadn't heard those words at all growing up. But Sebastiano made her feel both those things, and that made him even more dangerous than he'd been when they had been standing in front of the mirror. At least then she'd known her reaction to him was purely physical. This felt a whole lot deeper.

'You still have one wish left, you know. Have you decided what it is that you want?'

Poppy looked at him askance. 'You're asking me that now?'

'Why not?'

'Because...' She felt light-headed standing this close to him. 'Can I wish myself away from here right now?'

'I said it had to be within my power to deliver, *bella*.' His fingers stroked lightly across her jawline. 'That I cannot do without alarming everyone.'

'Then, no, I haven't.'

She shifted back a pace and his hand fell to his side. 'Is being here with me really that bad, Poppy?'

'No. Actually, it's not.' She made a face. 'Which is why I need pinching. I've never seen anything like this place and it feels like I've fallen into my very own fairy tale. And that only makes me feel worse, because it accentuates our differences.'

'I told you, whatever you want, I will get for you.'

'You don't get it, Sebastiano.' She shook her head. 'You can click your fingers and have anything you want. That's not real life for most people.'

His eyes cooled on hers. 'Actually, I learned a long time ago that you can't click your fingers and have whatever you want, which is why I work so hard. I make sure nothing will ever be taken away from me again.'

Aware that the conversation had deviated down a path they hadn't been down before, Poppy stared at him. She wanted to ask him what he was talking about but she was also aware that he had withdrawn from her and most likely wouldn't answer.

'Sebastiano, come sta? Tutto bene!' a disembodied male voice called from below.

Sebastiano turned to her. 'Ready?' he asked, his gaze hooded as he held his arm out for her once more. Nodding, Poppy descended the stairs beside him, aware of curious eyes turning to watch their progress.

A well-groomed Italian man with an air of confidence about him met them at the bottom of the stairs, a half-empty champagne flute in hand. His eyes did a slow tour of Poppy's figure. *'Chi e questa donna affascinante?'*

'Mine,' Sebastiano supplied smoothly. 'Poppy, this is a soon-to-be ex-friend of the family, Sergio Stavarone. Be careful; he is unattached and looking to receive a black eye.'

Sergio laughed and took her hand, kissing the back with a wicked glint in his eyes. 'Just say you don't want this ugly cretin, *bellisima*, and I am yours.'

Poppy grinned, she had no idea what he had said but his light-hearted banter seemed to ease Sebastiano's tension from moments ago. She caught the intense gleam in Sebastiano's gaze that said, *'Back off!'* to the debonair Italian and her stomach impersonated a tumble dryer.

'You're a really good actor,' she murmured as he led her to a part of the villa she hadn't been in before. 'I almost believed you myself back there.' Which would be to her detriment, she knew. 'Is this a ballroom?' Her astonished gaze swept the vast room lined with ornate mirrors and floor-to-ceiling windows facing the night-dark sea. Beautifully dressed men and women mingled while white-coated servants wove between them, offering drinks and finger food on silver trays.

'Yes, it is a ballroom.' Sebastiano grabbed two fluted glasses from a passing waiter, handing her one. 'And I wasn't acting. I didn't like the way he looked at you.'

'You're very possessive for a fake boyfriend,' she commented.

His eyes held hers. 'I'm very possessive full-stop.'

Poppy's heart did a little quickstep and she was very glad when a small group of well-turned-out Italians interrupted them. For some reason her defences regarding Sebastiano were lower tonight and, try as she might, she couldn't seem to find the wherewithal to resist his animal magnetism.

Knowing that could only lead to one outcome—a bad one—she decided to focus on the party and not the man beside her. It was a good idea, because she found that she actually enjoyed meeting and chatting with such a wide variety of people. Most of them were incredibly lovely, although one or two women shot daggers at her as they vied for Sebastiano's attention. Of course, he was a consummate fake boyfriend and played the part to perfection, always making sure she had a drink, including her in conversations and insisting that anyone who spoke to him did so in English. It was all a bit much, really.

Even so, there was often an undercurrent of something not quite right when some of the older Italians grabbed his attention.

After one particularly circumspect group departed, Poppy turned to him. 'Why does everyone treat you as if they haven't seen you in for ever?'

'Because they haven't.'

'Oh, well, that explains it,' she returned, deadpan. 'Seriously, though—that lovely couple before, for example, seemed awfully careful about what they said to you. It was almost as if they were walking on eggshells. The husband turned brick-red when he mentioned your parents and I thought his wife was going to stomp on his foot.'

'Don't you know, *bella*?' Sebastiano's teeth flashed white beneath the impressive chandeliers. 'I am the big, bad wolf. Or—what did you call me?—a shark.'

Poppy scoffed. 'You know I don't think that any more. I've seen your softer side and I'm not so easily fooled by your bad-boy exterior.'

'You are not only terrible for my ego, *bella*, but if I'm not careful my reputation as well.'

'Be serious,' she admonished. 'What am I missing?'

He raised his champagne flute to his lips. 'My mouth on yours.'

Poppy blinked, not sure she had heard him correctly. 'What did you just say?'

'I want to kiss you again, *bella mia*. Why do you look so shocked after the incredible kiss we shared yesterday?'

Poppy swallowed heavily. 'Because I am. That kiss was for show and—'

'Was the way your eyes ate me up back in my office that Sunday morning for show?'

Heat surged through her at the memory. 'My eyes did not eat you up.'

'I nearly kissed you then, you know,' he said almost conversationally. 'When your busy fingers were knotting my tie.'

'Sebastiano…'

'You know the only reason I told you to get me a shirt was to get your hands off me.'

'Well, I'm sorry if I over—'

'Because I was aroused.'

Poppy's breath caught in her lungs. His words were stripping away her more sensible side and rendering it obsolete.

He chuckled at her mute expression. 'You seem surprised.'

'I am. You date supermodels and beautiful actresses.'

'And now I date women who wear Mickey Mouse watches. I bet no one in my office put money on that.'

'No,' she agreed. 'But I knew I should have taken this off.' She fidgeted with the band. 'It's never looked so out of place before, but I forgot.'

Refusing to let her retreat behind her safe walls, Sebastiano curled his hand around her waist. 'Leave it on. It looks charming. Different. Original. You'll probably see a couture version selling on the Internet by morning.'

'I really don't think—'

'Poppy! Sebastiano! *Eccovi.* I have been looking for you everywhere.'

Poppy swung around at the sound of Giuseppe's voice, her eyes wide, her cheeks on fire. After listening to Sebastiano tell her how much he wanted her, all she could picture was her and Sebastiano's reflection in the mirror, his darker head bent to hers, his lips grazing her neck, his lean hands touching her. Stroking her.

'How are you enjoying the party?' his grandfather asked, clearly not picking up on the sexual tension that vibrated like a live wire between them.

'It's very good, Nonno,' Sebastiano answered for both of them, and Poppy was glad that he had, because she couldn't have strung a sensible sentence together if she'd tried.

Stunned by the strength of his need to enclose Poppy in his arms and lay claim to her, Sebastiano released her and shoved his hands deep into his pockets. He'd been trying to distract her from her perceptive questioning by telling her the effect she had on him but he'd only served to turn himself on. Big time.

Which wasn't like him. He never struggled to keep himself in check. He was always cool. Always in control. His grandfather would expect it. And yet here he was, about to ravish a woman he shouldn't even want. A woman, who despite her claims to the contrary, wanted him just as much but who would no doubt behave like every other woman he had bedded and want more from him in the end.

Even knowing that, he wanted her with a hunger that floored him. He wanted to claim her and soak up her softness. Soak up her goodness.

He took a deep breath. At some point over the last few days she had gone from not being his type to being the only woman he could think about. Even the beautiful Daria Perone, a woman he had wanted to bed for a long time but whose path he had never crossed at the right time, paled in comparison to the woman at his side. A fact she had reluctantly conceded earlier in the evening when he had introduced her to Poppy.

Poppy had known something was up by the way Daria's hungry eyes had lingered on him.

'I thought you said there would be no ex-girlfriend's here,' Poppy had said with her proud little nose in the air after Daria had sauntered off to find more easy prey.

Sebastiano had laughed. 'She's not an ex.'

'Oh.' Realisation had made her innocent blue eyes sparkle. 'Maybe she's heard you give really good kiss-off presents.'

She had fingered the pearl happily nestled between her round breasts, and he had wanted to pull her in close and never let her go.

Right now he'd like to end the evening early and take her to his bed. Stamp out the hollow feeling in his heart with her sweet body underneath his.

But his *nonno* had other ideas.

'Wait here,' his grandfather said, nodding to the musicians, who automatically stopped playing. 'I have an announcement that will make you happy, *nipote mio.*'

Sebastiano felt the blood move through his veins in a slow, dull thud when his grandfather took the microphone. Surely his grandfather wasn't going to make the announcement that he was going to take over CE here, tonight?

'Friends. Family. We are here tonight to celebrate *l'amore della mia vita.*' His grandfather gestured to Evelina who had come to stand beside him. He gave her a soft kiss and joined their hands together.

'What did he say?' Poppy whispered.

'The love of his life,' Sebastiano rasped.

He felt Poppy sigh beside him and his gut clenched. Yes, she would definitely want more from a man than he had it in him to give.

His grandfather waxed lyrical about his wife for a few more minutes to the avid enjoyment of the crowd. Then he held up his hand, his expression serious. 'And of course, most of you know that fifteen years ago on this night our family was dealt a cruel blow that we have struggled to overcome. It is fair to say that the intervening years have not been easy. But tonight…' His moist eyes scanned the crowd and locked with Sebastiano's. 'Tonight I want to create new, happier memories for all of us. So it is with great pleasure that I announce that my grandson, Sebastiano Castiglione, will be taking over as CEO of Castiglione Europa. Effective immediately.'

Sebastiano heard the applause and well wishes from the crowd but it sounded as if it came from far away. He had expected the announcement of his appointment to be more along the lines of a memo. A public statement written up by his PR people in a way that created little fanfare. The last thing he wanted was to be the centre of attention. Not tonight. Not when it should have been his father taking over this position instead of him.

Taking the dais to thunderous applause, he said a few words about his grandfather's non-existent retirement plans that lightened the air considerably, then he signalled to the musicians to start playing again.

Needing a drink, he raised his hand to those nearby in a gesture of thanks and made his way to the bar, the guests he passed giving him little more than a pat on the back and a, 'Well done, congratulations'.

'Scotch. Neat,' he grated at the hapless bartender who had a goofy grin on his face. The man's grin slipped a little as he quickly did what he was asked. In the blink of an eye, the drink was gone and Sebastiano slapped the now empty glass back down on the bar. 'Another.'

'Sebastiano...' Not realising that Poppy had followed him, he glanced at her. 'Sebastiano, your parents died today?'

'Please spare me the mini-violin, *bella*. I'm over it.'

She watched him, her blue eyes frankly appraising. 'Does anyone actually believe that when you say it?' she asked softly, sympathy leaching out of every one of her beautiful pores.

'Don't push, Poppy. Another,' he said to the hovering bartender.

Her mouth firmed into a stubborn line. 'Why are you drinking Scotch if you're so over it?'

'I like the taste.'

'Sebastiano...'

Deciding he needed air as well as Scotch, he pushed away from the bar. 'Excuse me, would you? There's someone I have to talk to.'

Moving past her, Sebastiano made his way out of the ballroom taking the stone steps down to the leafy garden. He had no idea where he was going, but being alone seemed like a good idea right now.

CHAPTER TEN

POPPY CAME AWAKE with a start and pushed herself into a sitting position. The sofa Sebastiano had slept on the night before was possibly the most uncomfortable piece of furniture she had ever fallen asleep on. Not that she had meant to fall asleep.

'Why aren't you in bed?'

She glanced across the room to find the cause of her disturbance silhouetted in the doorway. 'I was waiting for you.'

Sebastiano stepped into the room, closing the door behind him, enveloping them in semi-darkness, the floor lamp Poppy had put on the only light source in the room.

He strolled towards her with the loose-limbed grace of a professional marauder, his bow-tie swinging from his collar, his jacket tossed carelessly over his shoulder.

Dumping the jacket on a chair, he made his way to the drinks cabinet. 'Why?'

Poppy's heart thudded heavily inside her chest as he poured himself a drink. 'I wanted to make sure you were all right. It's what I would do if we were in a normal relationship.'

'Only we're not in a normal relationship,' he pointed out.

Poppy pushed her hair back from her face impatiently. 'Why do you get to pull that card out when it suits you but I can't?'

His lips twisted as if she amused him. 'Because I make the rules, intern, not you.' He tossed ice into the glass, not looking at her. 'You should go to bed.'

The fact that he'd called her 'intern' in his deep, sexy

voice set her insides ablaze. There was something so intimate and affectionate in the way he said it, although right now he probably hadn't meant it to sound either of those. 'And you should stop drinking,' she offered pleasantly.

'Where's the fun in that?'

Poppy stood up and smoothed her hand down her beautiful dress. 'Are you very drunk?'

His eyes skimmed her. 'Not nearly enough that I want to listen to your "good little girlfriend" act.'

Poppy pursed her lips. 'How about my bad one?'

His smile didn't quite meet his eyes. 'Now that one has potential.'

Poppy remembered everything he had said to her downstairs, every seductively appealing word he had uttered to prevent her from asking probing questions, and warned herself not to fall for his pretences again. The man was a ruthless shark, after all. 'Isn't your grandfather's announcement of you taking over CE supposed to have made you happy?'

Sebastiano smiled at her. 'You know, that's the strangest thing. It didn't.' He downed another finger of Scotch. 'Go figure.'

She crossed the floor and stood in front of him, her arms folded defensively across her chest.

'I was really angry with you for walking off and leaving me before but now...' She sighed. 'If I'd known about your parents I could have—'

'What?' His blank eyes met hers. 'Dressed me in flannel pyjamas and brewed me a pot of tea? Isn't that what you English do when you feel sorry for someone?'

Her mouth settled into a stubborn line. 'Maybe it would help if you talked about your feelings, Sebastiano, instead of pretending you don't have any.'

'You know, I spent most of last night wondering what you wear to bed and I couldn't decide if it would be silk.' He took a long slug of Scotch. 'Or cotton.'

'Don't,' Poppy said warningly. 'Don't pretend you want me to distract me. That trick might have worked once but only a fool would fall for it twice.'

'And you're no fool, are you, Poppy?'

'Sebastiano...'

'You're really very cute when you're riled. It turns me on immensely. In fact, everything about you turns me on, *bella*. Especially in that dress. *Por Dio*, but you look hot. Deliciously, sensually hot.'

Even though she knew he was toying with her, Poppy felt the warm flush of desire flow through her. Clearly her hormones did not require honesty as a prerequisite to arousal, and wishing it were otherwise wasn't going to change anything.

Especially since she suspected that Sebastiano's superficial guise was a way to keep the world at bay just as her sarcasm often achieved the same result. In that they were alike.

Disconcerted by that observation, she glanced up to find him watching her with a hunting stillness that caused her breath to back up in her lungs. The tension in his large frame was palpable and her pulse raced.

She shivered, doing her best to suppress the desperate ache that had bloomed deep inside her. Right now she could walk away from this fake arrangement unscathed. It was important that she remember that because, while her heart might think that throwing herself at Sebastiano was a great idea, her sensible side was of the opposite opinion.

Taking a deep breath, she zoned in on her sensible side. Anything was better than being at the mercy of her more dangerous, libidinous one that wanted nothing more than for her to throw herself at him.

'So is this what you normally do on the anniversary of your parents' deaths?' she queried lightly. 'Get drunk?'

Sebastiano held up his half-empty Scotch glass like a proud Boy Scout presenting a shiny new badge. Then he turned to refill it. 'I think your judgmental side is showing again, Miss Connolly.'

Ignoring his dig, Poppy moved closer. 'Wouldn't it be nicer to be with other people on a night like this? People who care about you? Like your family? A girlfriend?'

'Inviting a woman to my home for anything other than sex would undoubtedly give her the wrong message. I don't ever want someone to imagine that I might be her next meal ticket.'

Poppy rolled her eyes. 'I hate to point out the obvious, Sebastiano, but you've basically offered to be mine.'

'Ah, but not for life, *bella mia.*'

It was both a statement and a warning. A warning she'd do well to heed. She was merely a guest in this extraordinarily opulent land, not a resident. And that was a role she definitely knew how to play because no one had ever wanted her around for long.

Usually she would throw out a deflecting line about now to lighten the atmosphere, but she couldn't muster one up right now, because she knew this strong, capable man was hurting and all she wanted to do was ease his pain. 'I know what it's like to lose a parent, Sebastiano,' she said softly. 'I know how it hurts. How it makes you feel lost. Scared.'

Sebastiano poured himself another drink and settled back against the cabinet, watching the play of tender emotions cross Poppy's beautiful, unguarded face, pity being the prime emotion, and the last one he wanted to see.

He wasn't sure if she was aware of it but her tongue kept darting out to moisten her lips as if she was preparing for his kiss; his muscles automatically drew tight at the thought.

The best thing she could do for the both of them was to take herself off to bed and he knew exactly how to send her there. 'But do you know what it's like to *cause* their deaths?' he rasped, the words burning like vinegar in his throat.

Her stunned eyes met his and there was a touch of sadness in their depths. 'Sometimes I did wonder if my mother chose drugs over me because I wasn't nice enough,' she admitted softly. 'But, no, I don't in the way I suspect you're talking about. What happened?'

Unprepared for her to take his disclosure with such equanimity, Sebastiano answered before he thought better of it. 'I was a selfish little bastard who wanted to spend time with his new girlfriend rather than go on a holiday with my family, that's what happened.' He let out a harsh laugh. 'What I didn't realise at the time was that my new friends were more interested in my money and social connections, and when we were caught buying drugs my parents had to drive to Rome to collect me. They were upset, disappointed, but I was too self-righteous and embarrassed to apologise. Some time after that my father lost control of the car on the icy roads.' He swallowed heavily at the memory. 'I walked away unscathed. They didn't walk away at all.'

The blood pounded in his head and he hadn't realised she had moved so close to him until her scent drifted towards him. 'But you didn't walk away unscathed,' she murmured. 'You carry the pain here.' She laid her palm against his chest, directly over his heart. 'Don't you?'

Sebastiano swore softly, his emotions boiling over inside him. The deep core of ice he'd encased himself in for so long preventing him from whispering that she was right. He did carry the pain of that day in his heart and he never let himself forget what a little *bastardo* he had been.

He stepped back from her and came up against the drinks cabinet. 'I don't want your pity, Poppy.'

She stepped closer. So close he could see that betraying pulse beating like a trapped bird inside her throat. 'I wasn't offering it.'

His gaze lingered on her lips before rising to hers again,

and her breath gave that betraying little hitch that told him she was as aroused as he was right now.

Dio, how was that possible when he had just been talking about his parents.

His muscles drew tight with the need to touch her. His mind and body were at war about the right thing to do, and the searing-hot, blistering need to make her his.

His?

He shook his head to clear it. 'You should go to bed,' he advised silkily. The sooner she was there, the safer she would be from the darkness that wanted to engulf him.

Her nostrils flared as if she had just scented danger. But still she didn't move. 'I will if you stop drinking.'

If he stopped drinking he'd do more than wonder if she was wearing the thong he had bought to match the gown.

Turning his back to her, he poured another finger of Scotch and then swung back to lean against the cabinet, raising his glass in a self-mocking toast. Before it touched his lips, she reached out and took hold of it, staying it in mid-air.

Adrenalin fuelled by sexual arousal turned his voice rough. 'You need to go to bed, Poppy.'

When he didn't release the glass to her, she brought her other hand up and slowly peeled his fingers away one by one. Sebastiano's heart beat a primal rhythm in his blood, heat and need turning his muscles hard.

'Or what?' she asked, her voice low, the sexy cadence scoring his skin.

In one swift move Sebastiano straightened to his full height, turned her and backed her against the cabinet. 'Or I'll ruin you for any other man.'

Her breath hitched again, her gaze on his mouth. 'Maybe your grandfather is right, Sebastiano. Maybe it's time to create new memories tonight.' Her blue eyes looked as luminous as the pearl nestled between her pert breasts. 'Memories that conjure up pleasure rather than pain.'

'You want pleasure, *bella mia*, I've got pleasure.'

He jerked her against him, the impact of her soft body against his like drinking water after trawling through a hot desert for months on end. The press of her round breasts against his chest shut down his reasonable, cool brain and replaced it with a greedy hunger that pushed at the limits of his civility.

She stared up at him, her hands trembling as they slowly pulled the short lengths of his bowtie from around his neck. 'Sometimes you look at me as if you know how to give me more pleasure than I've ever experienced in my whole life,' she said on a breathless rush. 'I want that. I *need* that.'

A low growl rumbled out of his chest at her admission, and he scattered the pins in her hair when he fisted his hands in it, bringing her mouth to his. He kissed her the way he had wanted to kiss her all night. Hard and deep. '*Dio*, I want you,' he murmured. 'So much I ache.'

She moaned, her hands twisting around his neck, her hips lifting against his as if seeking something just out of reach.

Bending his knees a little, he pressed his erection between the juncture of her thighs, rewarded for his efforts when she opened her mouth wider, her tongue tangling with his.

Driven by a need he could neither explain nor resist, Sebastiano kissed his way down the tender skin of her neck. They were both unattached, consenting adults who wanted each other, and he was done fighting something that had started the minute he'd laid eyes on her.

She moaned softly, her hands moving over his chest, his sides, his back as she tried to shift even closer.

'Poppy.' Sebastiano swore under his breath as the need

to be inside her drove all else from his mind. 'I have to have you.'

'Yes, yes.' Her urgency drove his own and he released the snap holding her bodice in place, letting the twin sides fall so that only the iridescent pearl lay between her exposed breasts. Cupping her, he brushed the tips with his thumbs before leaning down to fasten his lips around one proud peak, laving it with his tongue.

She cried out and he hefted her higher, pressing her against the wall to hold her steady.

Some small semblance of sanity reached him and told him he couldn't take her here against a wall, and he clamped his mouth over hers as he carried her into the bedroom.

She lay dazed, spread out before him on the large bed, the silky fabric of her dress falling between her shapely thighs like a silver waterfall.

Breathing deeply, he yanked his shirt open, uncaring that buttons scattered over the carpet. Shucking out of it, his hands reached for his belt buckle and he stilled. His raging hard-on pressed against his zipper as he drank her in: her hair now tumbled from its sleek knot and spread around her; her naked breasts rosy and full; her slender arms raised in supplication above her head.

'You should come with a health warning,' he growled. 'One touch and you'll be changed for ever.'

Her eyes lifted to his, scorching a path up over his stomach and chest. 'That's you, not me.'

Her legs shifted together and he ran his hand along the outside of her thighs, gentling her. 'You're going to have to open these, *dolce mia*.' His eyes dropped to her legs. 'If you want me to take care of that ache.'

He came down beside her and she squirmed against him, her nails scoring his shoulders. Her movements were almost untutored; her soft pleas for more sounding as if she had never had a man touch her like this before.

Knowing that couldn't be the case in this day and age, Sebastiano reached for a condom and moved over her, his knee pressing high between her legs. 'You like that?' He nipped at the exposed skin above her hip, loving the way she moaned his name. 'When I press here.' He moved up to her breasts. 'When I suckle you there?'

'Yes. Please…' Her hands reached for him, smoothing over his shoulders, following the line of muscle either side of his spine.

Feeling as if he was about to possess something rare and unique, Sebastiano planted a soft, pre-emptive kiss beside her navel and dragged her gown down past her hips. It slithered to the floor but his eyes were riveted to the tiny white thong covering her femininity. His finger slid down the centre of the lace, his eyes trained on her face. She bit her lip to stop herself from crying out, her hips jerking upwards. He'd been right. She was all fire and wild passion, and now she was his. One-hundred-percent his.

'Sebastiano!' Her fingers dug into his scalp and she writhed against the moist kisses he planted along her collarbone, his fingers finding her slick and hot and ready. Her cry of pleasure as her body opened for his touch almost wrecked his self-control.

'Oh, yes, I know what you want.'

Nudging her legs apart, he ripped the thong from her body and rose above her. He settled between her thighs, latching on to a raspberry nipple as he pressed into the soft folds of her femininity, feeling her body give as it stretched to accommodate his.

Sweat broke out on his forehead as he eased inside her slick centre. She undulated against him, as if the pressure was too much, and he gave up trying to go slow and plunged deep, immediately stiffening as he felt her jerk beneath the power of his thrust.

Smoothing her hair back from her forehead, he took his

weight on his elbows, staring down at her. 'Poppy, *amore mia*, are you all right? Did I hurt you?'

She gazed up at him, a mixture of wonder and wariness in her gaze. 'I'm fine. It doesn't hurt...now.'

Sebastiano swore softly in Italian. 'Poppy was that...? Were you a virgin?'

She panted what sounded like a yes, her fingers digging into his lower back, her legs widening to take him deeper.

'Wait,' he ordered roughly. 'Let your body get used to mine.'

'Oh, that feels good again.'

Sebastiano growled under his breath. The cool part of his brain shrieked entrapment, but the primal, instinctive part overrode it, telling him to go deeper and harder in a mating ritual too powerful to ignore.

'Just relax, Poppy.' He groaned as she pressed upwards, his hands finding her hips to force her to go slow. 'Let me show you.'

She moaned softly as he pushed slowly into her, her arms clinging to him, her legs high around his waist to take him all in.

He whispered her name, petting her, watching her, learning what she liked. If sex had ever felt this good, he couldn't remember it. 'You're mine now, *bella*,' he growled. 'Mine.'

He brought her eyes to his, forging a deeper connection with her as he slowly started to move inside her, some primal part of him thrilling to the fact that he was her first.

'Sebastiano...' She hooked her ankles around his lean hips, her body straining for something no man had ever given her before.

'That's it, Poppy,' he murmured. 'Give yourself to me, let me pleasure you. I've got you, *dolce mia*, I've got you.'

'I can't... I don't think...' She panted his name and then he felt it, the moment her body tightened before flinging her into a mind-bending orgasm.

Sebastiano rode it out with her, holding her, soothing her, glorying in the wonderment shining out of her blue eyes.

The ripples of her body pushed at his self-control, making her soft and open for his possession. And Sebastiano did possess her, driven by the demons of his past and a woman who made him want more than any other... Then suddenly it was just her and him, and right before he found his own powerful release she wound her arms around his torso and held him tight with her whole body, sending him to a place he'd never been to before.

'Oh, my...' she murmured drowsily, her arms loosening their hold around his neck.

Sebastiano slipped from her body, his heart still pounding inside his chest.

She whimpered as he disposed of the condom, quickly returning to tuck her replete body against his side.

'That was your first time,' he said, trying to sort through the myriad emotions coursing through him. Disbelief. Pride. Wariness. *Contentment.*

His mind couldn't seem to decide how he was supposed to feel about taking Poppy's virginity but, damn it, he wished she had told him. 'You should have told me.'

'Mmm...' She snuggled closer against his side, one arm flung across his middle. 'I didn't think of it.'

'You didn't think of it?'

Now that he couldn't believe. How could a woman who was about to have sex for the first time not think of something so important?

'Well, I thought about it, but then...' She sighed with her whole body. 'Then I forgot until you pushed inside me.'

Just hearing those words on her lips made him hard again. He clenched his jaw. He didn't do virgins as a general rule—he'd never had a virgin before in his life—and the fact that Poppy had chosen him to be her first...

'Why me?' he asked softly, holding his breath as he waited for her answer.

When all that came was the soft, even sound of her breathing, he glanced down to find she had fallen asleep.

Fallen asleep?

That was usually his modus operandi, his body too sated to do anything but shut down. Only he wasn't sated right now, he was raring to go again, his brain trying to convince him that he could wake her up, roll her onto her back and slip inside her warm, welcoming body without any need for foreplay.

Emotions he couldn't—and didn't particularly want to— identify rolled through him. The night had been going well right up until his grandfather had made his speech and re- minded him all over again how he had stuffed up in his youth.

Feeling the old sense of remorse rise up in him again, he turned his head into Poppy's hair and inhaled her unique female scent, smoothing his fingers down her spine.

She shifted against him, sighing deeply, and he imme- diately felt calmer, as if she were the port his icy heart was seeking like a battle-weary ship caught in a storm.

Shaking his head at his uncharacteristically whimsical thoughts, he knew that only one thing here was true. Poetic.

Sex had been very effective at keeping his demons at bay.

CHAPTER ELEVEN

A PERSON SHOULD feel good the day after they reached a much-longed-for milestone. Great, even.

Sebastiano felt like crap. The only milestone his brain could focus on was the one that had been reached in his bed last night, and that one wasn't even his.

He told himself that if Poppy wasn't troubled about losing her virginity then he shouldn't be either. Unfortunately logic was in short supply right now and he scowled darkly as he sipped his rapidly cooling coffee and stared out at the slate-grey sea, almost indistinguishable from the sky above.

As far as he could tell, Poppy hadn't stirred from his bed yet and he wasn't completely surprised. He'd woken her twice during the night to have her again and he'd had to force himself to leave her before doing so again this morning. Only the notion that he wanted her a little too much for comfort, and the knowledge that she must be sore, drove him from the tangled sheets and out onto the sofa made of bricks.

Remembering how those sheets had become so tangled, and her soft cries of pleasure as he'd shown her what her body was made for, had him hardening once more like one of Pavlov's dogs on speed. It would be pointless to deny that he wanted more than one night with her, but his guard was up, and putting some emotional distance between them seemed like the best move he could make.

He hadn't meant to complicate their arrangement with sex, but what was he to do when she'd bailed him up against the drinks cabinet and told him she wanted to experience real pleasure?

The woman never stopped surprising him. But the last thing he wanted was for her to read more into last night than what it was—phenomenally hot sex—and, having been a virgin, she undoubtedly would. So he'd tread carefully and let her down gently. Not that his kindness made him feel any less of a bastard. The fact was, he'd taken advantage of their situation and now he had to deal with the consequences. Which made what he had to tell her when she woke up all the more complicated.

Hearing a noise behind him, he turned like a man about to face a firing squad.

Maledizione. What was wrong with him? So he'd stuffed up—again. Time to take it like a man.

'Hi.'

Her soft, almost shy smile told a thousand stories and he knew none he'd want to hear. She wanted more. More than he could ever give. His gaze raked down over her thin cotton dressing gown. His heart lurched. She looked sleep-mussed and utterly beautiful. 'You're awake.'

Way to go, Castiglione; state the obvious, why don't you?

'Sort of.' She touched her hair self-consciously. 'I'm not a morning person.'

'That's good, because morning finished about a half an hour ago.'

'Really?' She glanced around searchingly, presumably for her watch or phone. 'My body clock is all out.'

He frowned. 'Because you're usually just finishing up a late shift?'

'Mmm... I suppose. Is that coffee hot?'

'Yes.' He poured her a cup and she moaned with pleasure at the first sip. 'Thanks.'

'You're welcome.'

They were acting like polite strangers and he found it

impossible to get a read on her. Normally a woman would be wrapping herself around him about now and telling him how wonderful he was.

'So.' She broke the growing silence between them. 'What happens now?'

'Usually...' Sebastiano began, wanting to shake up her insouciance when he had taken her damned virginity last night. 'I take the woman I'm with back to bed,' he continued softly. 'And repeat everything that happened the night before. Several times.' It was a lie. Usually he couldn't wait to go for a run and get to the office. Except this morning it wasn't true. This morning he'd happily drag her back through that door and repeat the night they'd just shared ad infinitum.

'Oh.' Her eyebrows rose. 'No wonder that woman was crying on the phone.'

It took him a minute to place her comment and when he did he shook his head. 'Why do you never say what I'm expecting you to say?'

Poppy sucked in a deep breath and let it out slowly.

It was no great feat to guess what Sebastiano was thinking. He'd given in to the emotion—and alcohol—last night and slept with her, and now he regretted it. No doubt he regretted telling her about his parents too, but at least she understood him a little better now. Understood that he carried guilt and pain around for his part in their deaths, but really, he'd only been a normal teenager rebelling against the bounds of his parents' restrictions. It was something she could easily imagine Simon doing. That it had ended in such tragedy was a tragedy in itself.

Given that last night had been the anniversary of their deaths, she was under no illusion that had another woman offered herself to him he would have chosen her to ease his burden instead. Poppy had just been in the right place at the right time—or not, depending on how you viewed it.

And she refused to view it as a bad thing. How could she, after the way he had made her feel? He was every woman's dream man. And not because of his money, as he thought, but because of his strength, his determination, even his arrogance. He was the kind of man a woman could rely on, if he ever chose to let one get close enough to fall in love with her.

A lump formed in her throat. For a while in his arms the night before her world had seemed perfect. He had been perfect. Caring. Considerate. Passionate. He had made her feel like the most beautiful woman in the world and she couldn't regret that. No doubt it was how he made every woman feel.

Okay, time for her to get back to the reality of her life. And the reality was that the only thing she could rely on with any degree of certainty was herself. Life was harsh and people could be brutal. Why open yourself up to that kind of pain unnecessarily, as her mother had done over and over?

And clearly Sebastiano's polite stranger routine was his way of trying to avoid a nasty scene between them now. But she had no intention of bawling him out, or blaming him for last night. After all, she had slept with him willingly, and she would put him out of his misery and show him that she was not going to be one of his women who clung and begged him to love them.

A tight, invisible band formed around her chest as if of their own accord her ribs had contracted to hold everything inside.

'So I think it's safe to say,' she began amicably, 'That last night was a mistake, don't you?'

'You're damned right it was a mistake.'

'Okay then…' She hadn't expected him to agree quite so vehemently but, whatever; *move on*.

He ran a hand through his already tousled hair. 'What I meant to say was that I don't bed virgins.'

'Okay—I'm not sure how to respond to that.' She gave a small laugh. 'Do you want an apology?'

'No I do not want a damned apology,' he grated. 'Damn it, Poppy, what kind of game are you playing? Why didn't you tell me?'

'Didn't we already cover this off last night?'

'Not to my satisfaction.'

Poppy expelled a pent-up breath. 'Look, Sebastiano, I'm not great at the whole morning-after thing so—'

'That would be because it's your first.'

'Right.' She cleared her throat. 'Another one. Okay—' she held her hand up as he glowered at her '—I don't know why this is such a big deal for you. It was my virginity to give away. And if you're worried that I'll expect more from you than one night, rest assured that I don't.'

'I could have hurt you.'

'I think we covered that off too…'

'And we'll cover it off again until I'm satisfied.' He growled. 'Are you sore?'

She was, but it was such a pleasurable ache it made her want to do everything they had done to cause it all over again. 'I'm fine, Sebastiano, but clearly you're not. And I think it's because you're afraid that I'm going to fall for you and start demanding rings and pre-nuptial agreements.' His jaw tightened. 'It's tempting,' she said with a slight laugh. 'But I promise you I won't. I know what this is, and if there's one thing I excel at its temporary relationships. Especially fake ones.' She'd meant that last to be humorous, but he wasn't laughing.

Thankfully her phone chimed a message and she dove on it like a seagull on a salted chip, a soft smile curling her lips when she read the name on the screen. 'It's Maryann,' she said, as if he would want to know. 'She and Simon are feasting on pancakes and ice-cream.'

Her eyes shone just thinking about them and she realised

how much she looked forward to seeing Simon and giving him a hug. 'What time should I tell them we'll be returning? You said yesterday it would be in the morning but I guess we've missed that time slot. Although I would like to take a shower if there's time.'

'There's time.'

He stared at her, brooding, and Poppy forced herself to smile. An hour to get ready, two to fly to London, another hour in traffic and maybe, just maybe, after that her shoulders would no longer be pinned up around her ears. 'Great.'

'Because we've hit a snag.'

Her eyes narrowed. 'A snag?'

'A problem,' he clarified. 'It seems my grandfather organised a business meeting in Venice later this week but it's been moved to tonight.'

'Okay.'

'Since I'm the new CEO, and the guy happens to be a friend of mine, I have to take the meeting.'

Poppy couldn't see any problem with that. 'Well that's great, isn't it? It's what you wanted. Control of your family's company.'

'Yes, but you have to come with me.'

'Me? I'm heading back to London.'

'You *were* heading to London, *now* you're heading to Venice. For a night.'

Poppy's lips went dry. 'But it's a Sunday.' Exactly a week since they'd met. 'I only know one person who works on a Sunday.'

He gave her a sardonic look and she crinkled her nose.

'I was only working that day because I had something to finish up. Usually I'm home studying, or sleeping.'

'Well, tonight you're dining at Harry's Bar. It's the only time Lukas has free, and I need to capitalise on the negotiations my grandfather started with his company six months ago.'

'You know I could just fly back to London on a commercial flight. I don't mind.'

'I do. And how will it look to my grandparents if you don't go with me? Especially since Lukas is bringing his wife.'

'Like I'm busy and have my own life.'

'We agreed on the weekend, *dolce mia*, and it's still the weekend.'

Poppy gave an exasperated sigh. 'You know, you're like one of those enormous earth-movers when you want something.'

'What can I say? It's my best trait.'

Poppy instantly thought about all the things he had done to her body last night. 'I wouldn't say that,' she murmured, excusing herself before he saw her face flame with embarrassment.

'Poppy?'

She turned back to look at him.

'If your reticence about Venice is because you think I'll expect a repeat performance after last night, you're wrong. I've already organised a suite with two rooms for tonight.'

Poppy let out a soft breath. Sadly, after his polite stranger routine this morning she hadn't thought that he would want anything from her, let alone a repeat performance.

'Does anyone ever say no to you?' she asked quietly.

'Only you, *bella*. Only you.'

But she didn't say no to him all the time, and she was very much afraid that if he touched her once more she wouldn't say no to him again.

'So, who is the guy again? Lukas Kursnet—Lukas Kornis—'

'Kuznetskov.' Sebastiano guided her out of the small launch and onto the red-carpeted jetty in front of the palatial Cipriani Hotel. Poppy was wide-eyed as she stared up at the blush-coloured Moorish building that rose out of the water like an elegant apparition.

They had arrived in Venice just over two hours ago, the city's unique beauty captivating and seducing her from the first glimpse of its elegant, centuries old architecture.

She smiled at the liveried hotel employee as she moved towards the main entrance. 'And his wife, Eleanore, you said? They're in shipping, right?'

'Lukas started in shipping and expanded into hotels. Eleanore runs her own consulting and design business.' Sebastiano's hand brushed her lower back as they passed through the incredible foyer towards the main restaurant. 'But relax, intern, I'm not going to grill you on this later.'

'That's a rel— Say, is that Julia Roberts?'

'Who?'

'The actress— Oh, never mind, I was probably wrong anyway.' She smoothed down the knee-length skirt of her silky dress and gazed around her in wonder. 'I'm just glad I lowered my pride and borrowed one of the dresses you bought at the start of the weekend. I thought the beautiful guests at your grandparents' party were intimidating but the women here could give a girl a complex for life.'

'You look stunning. You always look stunning.'

His low voice brought her eyes to his. He was wearing a suit with an open-neck shirt and he looked so handsome he made her heart ache. For all her good intentions on the flight to Venice—simply to enjoy a night in another exotic city and treat Sebastiano as if he were just any other man— she wasn't succeeding very well. 'Thanks. So do you.'

He stared down at her and Poppy willed her racing heart rate to settle. It would be mortifying if he realised that, far from thinking last night had been a mistake, she had in fact spent the day thinking about his impressive naked body. And no amount of internal pep talks about his 'love 'em and leave 'em' attitude towards women seemed to make a spit of difference to her treacherous hormones.

Suddenly he reached out to tug a strand of her hair away from where it had caught on her lip gloss and Poppy's breath backed up in her lungs. The way he was looking at her right now, she would swear he didn't think last night had been a mistake either.

'Castiglione.' A man cleared his throat behind them.

'Ah, Lukas... Eleanore.' Sebastiano turned to the couple as if the moment they had just shared had never happened. 'You look lovely as usual.' Sebastiano gave the requisite double kisses to the woman's cheeks. 'This is Poppy Connolly. Poppy, may I present Eleanore and Lukas Kuznetskov?'

'Harrington,' Eleanore corrected with a smile.

'Really?'

Clearly surprised Sebastiano glanced at Lukas who merely shook his head. 'Don't ask.'

Eleanore laughed delightedly at the men's wry grins and Poppy felt a bubble of happiness well up inside her as she watched the glamorous couple—Lukas with his dark-blond hair and striking blue eyes, and Eleanore with her cat-like elegance and wide smile. They looked relaxed and at ease with each other as if they had been together forever. Poppy knew MaryAnn would have taken one look at them and said, 'True love.'

'Poppy, it's lovely to meet you,' Eleanore said with genuine warmth. 'I'm so glad you could join us. Is this your first visit to Venice?'

'Yes, it is.'

'Mine too,' Eleanore said. 'I love it. You?'

'It's magical.'

'Exactly the word Eleanore used when we landed,' Lukas said, giving his wife an indulgent smile. 'Hello, Poppy, I'm the luggage handler.'

Poppy laughed, already liking this couple immensely.

'Oh, you're more than that,' Eleanore assured him. 'You organise incredible sleigh rides too.'

Lukas flushed at the in joke and Sebastiano gave a low laugh at the other man's discomfort. Groaning, Lukas shook his head. 'See what married life does to you, Castiglione? It breaks you.'

Eleanore elbowed her husband in the ribs. 'Stop complaining; you love it.'

Lukas's eyes gleamed, as if he wanted to show her just how much he loved it, and Poppy found herself entranced.

'I don't know about you lot,' Sebastiano interjected suavely, 'But the last meal I ate was pizza about—was it yesterday or the day before?' he asked Poppy.

Poppy shook her head. 'I swear men are born with hollow stomachs. My brother is exactly the same.'

'My sister Olivia eats like a horse,' Eleanore said. 'I was always so jealous growing up because she never put on a pound.'

'Table. Conversation,' Lukas instructed, guiding his wife with a hand at the small of her back. 'I think my last meal was yesterday as well.'

Eleanore, it turned out, was incredibly creative and had dabbled in art classes when she'd been younger, informing Lukas that they would be visiting the Gritti Palace some time the following day after Poppy had gushed about the Byzantine artwork in the foyer.

Poppy thought that Lukas would quite possibly fly to the moon and wrangle a star back for Eleanore if she was so inclined.

True love indeed, she mused, unconsciously taking in how relaxed the other couple was with each other—the covert touches, the possessive way Lukas leaned his arm along the back of Eleanore's chair and the soft glow in his eyes when he looked at her. Just being with them made her feel warm and included.

Included?

Yes, she felt included. Like she had with Sebastiano's family, as if she actually had a valuable contribution to make to the order of things.

A lump formed in her throat and she blinked back a shimmer of tears that was forming behind her eyes. If Sebastiano had asked her for her third wish right now, it would be to make this moment last for ever. Or maybe to make last night last for ever.

She was falling for him, she realised on a frantic rush of understanding, falling hard and fast, and she knew the landing would definitely not be soft this time.

Feeling unaccountably panicked, Poppy scraped back her chair and excused herself to go to the ladies' room. She had been the one to call last night a mistake, and he'd agreed, hadn't he?

'Hey, wait up.' Poppy nearly groaned to hear Sebastiano behind her. She stopped in the smoky corridor that led to the bathrooms but didn't look up at him. 'Are you okay?'

'Great,' she said, pinning a bright smile on her face.

'Really?' His intense gaze probed hers.

No! She was terrible. Panicked. Scared. 'Of course.'

'Poppy...'

'Sebastiano, don't.'

The last thing she wanted was for him to know how she felt and pity her. It would make her feel too pathetic for words.

His hands lifted to frame her face, bringing her eyes up to his. His nostrils flared as if he was drawing her scent into his body. She felt him shudder and then something came over his face. A softness. A sort of giving in. 'I want you.' The words sounded as though they'd been wrenched from a deep part of him and Poppy's traitorous heart started to sing. 'I know you said last night was a mistake but for me it was like nothing I've ever experienced before. You walk into a room, Poppy, and my body salivates to have you. You're like a drug. You're under my skin.'

Poppy stared up at him, incredulous, her mind barely able to register what she was hearing. 'I want you too,' she admitted huskily.

A woman glanced at them curiously as she made to move past and Sebastiano dragged Poppy closer against him. Then his mouth was on hers, open and demanding, and leaving her in no doubt as to how much he wanted her.

When they were jostled by a second person, Sebastiano raised his head with a groan. He looked at her. Took a deep breath. 'You need to fix your lipstick, *bella*,' he said gruffly. 'I'll meet you back at the table.'

'I like her.'

Sebastiano glanced at Lukas. The man's eyes were trained on Eleanore as she left the room to take a phone call. 'I hope so. You married her.'

'Interesting.' Lukas chuckled, giving him a look. 'Deflecting with humour. I had thought it was just casual between the two of you. Thanks for the clarification.'

Sebastiano narrowed his eyes. Frankly he was still reeling from what had just happened with Poppy in the corridor. He hadn't meant to say any of those things to her, they'd just spilled out and he certainly didn't need his old friend digging at him. 'Just because you're now married off, Kuznetskov, don't try and ruin it for the rest of us.'

'Safety in numbers and all that?' the Russian mused.

'Exactly. But there's nothing going on between Poppy and myself.' That was if you discounted last night and that savage kiss in the corridor just now. *Dio mio*, he could really pick his moments.

'Could have fooled me.'

'It's true,' he said, tossing an olive into his mouth. 'She was my intern and she helped me out of a tight spot.' Another olive. 'The important thing is that you'll be dealing with me from now on instead of my grandfather—and fair warning, but I'm about to fleece you so that we're the only contractor you use on your hotels in the foreseeable future.' He leaned back in his chair and raised his glass to his friend. 'What more could a man want?'

Lukas gave a helpless shrug. 'Poppy Connolly?'

Sebastiano scowled. 'Look, Kuznetskov, while I'm very pleased love has worked out for you not all of us want the same thing, or need it.' His scowl deepened as those words suddenly had a hollow ring to them. 'Personally, I'm not interested in capping my batting average just yet.' Or ever!

'Here, here,' Lukas drawled, raising his beer in a toast. 'So you won't mind if I get her number and text it to a few of my single friends?'

'Don't be an ass,' Sebastiano said. 'I doubt she'd have time to see any of your friends anyway.'

Not with the amount of nights she worked. Which bothered him immensely. He hated the idea that Poppy had to work nights to make ends meet. Damn it, that third wish of hers better be for ten million pounds or he was going to give her a piece of his mind.

'Castiglione?'

Unaware that he had started drumming his fingers on the table, Sebastiano frowned. 'Sorry, I missed that.'

Lukas smiled. 'I asked when you wanted to come to St Petersburg to go over the plans for the hotel restoration at Prospekt Avenue.'

'I'll touch base with the Head of Marketing as soon as she's back from New York and let you know.'

Sebastiano only faintly heard Lukas's reply, his eyes trained on Poppy as she wove her way towards them between the tables.

'By the way, I highly recommend it.'

Sebastiano stared blankly at the slow grin that spread across Lukas's face. 'Recommend what?'

'Married life.'

Mouthing a rude word, Sebastiano pulled Poppy's chair out for her as she sat down. Fortunately his friend didn't labour the point about marriage and the conversation resumed an easy flow.

The whole night had been easy, he realised. Poppy fitted in beautifully with the other couple. Not that Sebastiano had thought she wouldn't—but he'd just never done the double date thing before. Usually he met a woman, took her for a meal then back to either his place or hers where they had sex and went their separate ways, the pattern continuing until one or the other tired of it.

Sebastiano frowned. Running a global operation as successful as his meant a lot of contact hours, which didn't leave much down time.

Even nights out with male friends usually revolved around work. He rarely had time to indulge in boring chit-chat and yet that was exactly what tonight had morphed into. But it hadn't been boring. In fact, it had been relaxing and highly enjoyable.

His eyes ate up the woman at his side. It had been enjoyable because of Poppy Connolly. She was smart, caring, challenging, and the most sexually responsive woman he had ever known.

Which was when it hit him that his end goal had shifted without him even being aware of it. This was no longer about him trying to convince his grandfather that their relationship was real, it was about—it was about... He frowned. He had no idea what it was about; he just knew that he wanted her again.

He brooded over that, unable to take his eyes from Poppy's mouth as she devoured her ice-cream dessert, enjoyment evident every time she licked the spoon clean.

She chose that moment to look at him, her eyes darkening as she caught his gaze. 'Want some?'

She held the spoon out and his eyes never left hers as he dipped his head and sucked the ice-cream inside his mouth. Her eyes darkened even more, her long lashes lowering to mask the desire he'd already registered.

A strange sensation fluttered inside his chest.

He had always believed that true happiness was something he would never feel again but it welled up inside him, unexpected and full. A tentative, bubbling brook that scared him as much as it ensnared him.

'Okay, lovebirds,' Lukas drawled, breaking their connection and causing Poppy to blush. 'Time for us to hit the sack.'

'Lukas!' Eleanore whacked his shoulder with her clutch bag. 'Please excuse my husband, Poppy,' Eleanore implored with dignity. 'He's not usually so rude.'

'Not at all. It's been amazing meeting you both. I had a wonderful night.'

Sebastiano pushed his chair back. 'Time for us to go too, *bella.*'

CHAPTER TWELVE

SETTLING HIS HAND at Poppy's lower back, Sebastiano led her to the main foyer. 'Wait here while I order a water taxi.'

A thrill raced up Poppy's spine at the thought of returning to their hotel room. A thrill she needed to find some way to contain. Her intention to keep her heart safe from Sebastiano had gone up in smoke as soon as he had kissed her again. But it didn't change anything, did it? He only wanted her physically while she…she… *Was she really falling in love with him?*

No. She couldn't be. She was just doing the age-old thing of confusing lust with love even though she thought she knew better.

Confident that she could handle whatever this night brought without falling into her mother's trap of thinking that a man wanted more from her than he did, Poppy glanced around the opulent space, her eyes lingering on two fashionably dressed women with wistful smiles on their faces.

Wondering if they had recognised a celebrity of some sort, Poppy followed the line of their stares to find that it was Sebastiano who had captured their appreciative gazes.

No doubt they were noting the powerful width of his shoulders beneath his dinner jacket, the thick curl of his hair that would soon need a trim and those piercing green eyes he had just turned her way.

Poppy's breath stalled as his lips curved into a lazy smile, his gaze raking down over her in a slow burn.

Was there ever a man so gloriously male? So sensually

appealing? No doubt he'd had so many women give themselves to him, just as she had done, that he couldn't even remember their names.

She noticed one of the women eyeing her suspiciously, the other more openly hostile.

Don't worry, ladies, she wanted to say. *I know how just the look of him makes a woman's heart skip a beat but he'll be back on the market soon.*

And in real life they were exactly the type he would choose. Beautiful. Refined. Elegant.

A dismal feeling jolted inside her chest. By contrast, she was just an ordinary girl who had stumbled into an extraordinary situation.

Poppy watched him walk towards her, his stride powerfully male, sexual intent etched into every long, measured stride. For a moment she felt real fear invade her limbs. Everything inside her said that this couldn't end well. That it *wouldn't* end well.

'Ready, intern?'

He planted himself in front of her, shutting out the world behind him. She knew on some level that she was mad to put herself in the way of this freight train but she also knew that she would.

Not trusting that her voice wouldn't tremble when she spoke, she nodded, letting Sebastiano usher her outside to their waiting water taxi.

Excitement coursed through her and she turned her face up to the soft fall of snowflakes that fell softly like confetti from the sky. 'Oh,' she breathed. 'How magical.' Impulsively she curved her arm through Sebastiano's, snuggling close. 'Can we walk?'

'Walk?' Sebastiano looked at her as if she'd just asked him to swim.

'Yes.' She laughed at his pained expression. 'Please, Bastian. It's so beautiful with the snow falling all around us and I don't know if I'll ever make it back to Venice again.'

Sebastiano bit back a curse, sexual need pushing him to get her back to the hotel as quickly as possible. 'Of course.'

He fell into step beside her, an easy silence enfolding them as the enchantment of Venice wrapped them in its hazy black magic.

'Where are we?' she asked, looking around.

'Venezia,' he drawled.

'You do have a sense of humour.' She laughed, punching his shoulder lightly. Sebastiano smiled, enjoying the comfortable feeling between them.

'Are you warm enough?'

'Yes. And I meant *where* in Venice?' She pressed closer to his body and he tucked her against his shoulder. 'Where does this lane lead to?'

She pointed over a small wooden bridge and down a dimly lit alleyway. Sebastiano shrugged. 'Let's find out.'

They wandered aimlessly, traversing a series of narrow storybook canals and tiny lanes with elaborate shop fronts below lighted apartments, the smell of the sea heavy in the night air.

'Oh, that's a beautiful building.'

'The Peggy Guggenheim Museum,' Sebastiano said. 'It has a wonderful sculpture garden at the back.'

'The Nesher Garden,' Poppy provided. 'Eleanore said they have a new controversial artwork. It sounds interesting.'

'Want to take a look?'

'I'd love to, but it's closed.'

Sebastiano palmed his phone. 'Not to us.'

'What are you doing?' She pulled his arm downwards. 'You can't possibly think of trying to get it open.'

'Why not?'

'It's midnight and—' She shook her head. 'Could you?'

'Of course. CE did the restoration work on the building a few years back. On top of that, we are key patrons.'

Poppy shook her head. 'That's great, but put your phone away. We don't have to disturb the poor curator, or whoever would have to wake up to open the doors. We can see it tomorrow.'

Pocketing his phone, he turned to her, giving her a look she couldn't mistake. 'I might already have plans for tomorrow.'

'Such as?'

Her soft whisper was like the sirens' lure Odysseus would have warned his sailors to ignore. It heated his blood and called to that most primitive, that most male, part of him. The part that wanted to take her right here up against a stone bridge.

He sucked in a deep breath, misty air mixed with strains of Poppy. He slipped his arm around her waist and drew her closer. Her breath hitched and she whispered his name.

Another call. Another lure to his senses. He stared down at her beautiful upturned face, her flushed cheeks, her snow-damp hair.

His arms tightened around her, his nostrils flaring as he looked at her. 'Such as plans to inspect an important work of art of my own.'

'Really?' Another breathy whisper that hung on his senses. She arched towards him just a little, her breasts rising between them as if seeking the palms of his hands. 'What kind of art work?'

'Mmm…' Sebastiano leant close, inhaling her but not yet touching her; torturing them both. 'It's soft and curvy.' He demonstrated with the sweep of his hands. 'And it has these hidden valleys and wonderful peaks.'

Unable to help himself, he cupped one of those masterful peaks, moulding her in his hand, soaking in her soft moans of pleasure.

'It sounds—wonderful.' Her hands drifted over his arms and shoulders. Stroking. Petting. 'I wouldn't mind exploring myself.'

'Oh, yes, *dolce mia*.' He groaned. 'I have much that you can explore.'

And then he kissed her. Deeply. Drawing tiny cries of pleasure from her throat, murmuring to her in Italian, urging her to give him more. To give him everything. Again a pesky voice in his head said, *mine*, and his body tightened with need.

'Bastian, I want...' Poppy widened her legs and he slid his thigh between them. 'Oh yes, that. Right there.'

'Yes, Poppy,' he breathed against her mouth. 'Tell me what you want. What you need.'

Because he didn't know what he needed, apart from filling her body with his until he couldn't think. Until this intense hunger to make her his drove out this feeling that something was missing from his life.

Missing?

His life was full. Complete. There was nothing missing. And yet he couldn't deny the nagging sense that something definitely was.

Her?

The unbidden thought was almost enough to have him pulling back but then she moaned and twisted higher against him, her teeth grazing his jaw.

He should have shaved, he realised, so that he wouldn't mark her pale skin. And as soon as the thought entered his head it was all he wanted to do: mark her. Fill her. *Brand* her.

'Sebastiano, please...'

Uncaring as to where they were, Sebastiano firmed his hand over her bottom and urged their lower bodies together.

Minutes passed where all they did was kiss, tasting each other until he was so hard he was about to disgrace himself.

'Enough playing.' Sebastiano growled, having indulged her desire to walk long enough. 'We need to take this indoors before we get locked up.'

'I don't want to wait,' she moaned. 'I'm so desperate for you.'

'The feeling is mutual, *bella*, believe me.'

'*Buonasera, signor, signorina.* Gondola ride?'

Dazed with desire, Sebastiano turned to focus on the smiling gondolier in the stupid shirt and dark trousers. No, he did not want a damned gondola ride, he wanted a bed, wall, floor—any flat surface—but he knew, as soon as he heard Poppy's happy sigh, that he was thwarted again.

'When we finally get back to our hotel room,' he warned, 'You better be wet and ready for me because I won't be waiting.'

He turned to the gondolier and bared his teeth.

'Can you take us to the Gritti Palace?' he asked, hoping his voice revealed his desire for haste.

'*Si, si. Salire a bordo.* Come aboard.'

'Thank you.' Poppy's eyes shone in the hazy moonlight. 'This is so magical.' She turned in the curve of Sebastiano's arms. 'I love it.' She reached up and kissed him. It lacked the heat of her previous kisses but the sweetness of it lingered along with a sense of utter satisfaction. He slung his arm around her shoulders and pulled her in close.

'You want a song, *signor*? *Signorina?*'

'No.'

'Yes.'

Sebastiano sighed and Poppy laughed.

'Yes,' he amended gruffly.

The gondolier grinned, starting a low, melodic tune he became completely caught up in as the little boat rocked gently beneath tiny arched bridges and passed softly lit, enchanting buildings.

Poppy burrowed closer to him, her body replete as it

rested against his, as if they had already made love. But they hadn't and yet he felt just as contented as if they had. He felt…he felt… He frowned. What did he feel? A sense of rightness? A sense of—happiness? The realisation was like the unfurling of a corpse flower after a decade of dormancy. Something had been going on with him since he'd agreed to come to Italy, something he couldn't put a name to yet, but he would. He absolutely would.

'By the way.' Poppy turned her face up to his, a secret smile on her lips. 'I already am.'

Sebastiano's gaze lingered on her mouth. 'Already what?'

'Wet,' she whispered impishly.

'You are in so much trouble when we get back to our room, Miss Connolly,' he warned menacingly, turning her towards him and slipping his hand along her thigh.

'Stop that,' she admonished softly, checking to see if the gondolier had noticed his hand move beneath her skirt.

Of course, the man was too discreet for that.

'We are here, *signor.*'

Grazie a Dio!

'Bene,' Sebastiano said, deftly lifting Poppy out of the gondola, and paying the gondolier who knew what amount.

Poppy's face was flushed, her eyes fever-bright as they ran over his arms and chest, her gaze making him burn hotter than the sun.

Whisking her through the double doors the concierge held open, Sebastiano let her precede him into the narrow confines of the hotel lift. He followed her in, barely pausing to insert the keycard for their floor before pressing her flat against the back wall, angling her head to the side to kiss the breath from her body.

Her bottom pressed into his groin, her mouth opening wide beneath his, hungry and sweet. Sebastiano groaned. He wanted her. *Dio,* but he wanted her.

His hands slipped beneath the hem of her dress, raising it along the outside of her thighs as he stroked her stocking-clad legs.

'These have to go.' His fingers came into contact with sheer tights, the cloth tearing easily beneath his rough fingers. He groaned her name as he came into contact with warm baby-soft skin. He flattened her against the wall, pressing into her. 'You feel fantastic. So damned sexy.'

The lift juddered to a halt and Sebastiano shot his hand against the wall to steady them both, his breathing ragged. 'Room. Now.'

Once inside, he shucked out of his jacket and threw off his shirt.

'You are so magnificent,' she murmured huskily, stepping forward to comb her fingers through the smattering of hair on his chest. 'I wanted to run my hands over you that morning in your office.'

'Do it now,' he commanded, reaching around to slide the zipper of her dress down, going stock-still when she leant forward to press her lips against his pectoral muscles.

They clenched and he felt her smile against his skin. 'I like that you're so hard everywhere.'

Her lips drifted over his nipples and his breath rasped in his throat as she licked him. He forked his fingers in her hair, holding her lightly, letting her explore, but only just. Her lips drifted lower, tracking the trail of hair down the centre of his body, a trail that ended at his throbbing erection.

'Poppy…' He grabbed her arms and held her in front of him. 'I need you, *bella*. Desperately.'

With swift, unsteady movements he divested her of her dress and scooped her into his arms, his lips finding hers.

As soon as he reached the bed he dropped her onto it and came down over the top of her, clamping his mouth over one of her gorgeous little nipples and feasting on it.

She cried out, music to his ears, and he didn't hold back from delving his hand between her legs, moaning deep in his chest as he found her wet and swollen.

'Poppy, *amore mia*...' Senses overloaded, Sebastiano moved lower, peppering her silky abdomen with soft, open-mouthed kisses as he settled his shoulders between her thighs, urging them wider still.

'Sebastiano, I haven't—' Her hands lowered to hold him off and he kissed the backs of her hands.

'Now you want to be shy?'

'I'm not shy.' She moaned as he flicked her with his tongue. 'But this is so intimate.'

'More intimate than when I'm inside you?'

'Yes, if you must know.'

He laughed softly. 'You're so sexy, Poppy *mia*.' He gently shifted her hands and placed them on the bed beside her hips. 'When it gets too much for you, grab the sheets.'

His nose nuzzled her silky mound. 'You're beautiful, Poppy. Like the Venus de Milo come to life.' His mouth drifted lower. 'Perfect here...' He inhaled deeply. 'And here where you're soft and wet and waiting for me to fill you up.' He licked her, moaning his pleasure at her taste. 'Mine,' he said, the word rumbling from deep inside his chest. 'You're mine.'

CHAPTER THIRTEEN

HOURS LATER THE pale light of the winter sun washed over Poppy, disturbing her sleep. Again she woke alone, the sheets beside her cool to the touch. Feeling a pang of anxiety, she reminded herself that Sebastiano was an early riser and she pulled on the hotel robe and belted it lightly, her feet quiet as she crossed the carpeted floor.

She found him outside on the small stone terrace, the faint strains of the dawn sun shimmering off the silvery green canal. The sky beyond looked clear, but it was the man filling the small space that took all of her attention.

A cold breeze ruffled his thick, dark hair and she remembered tunnelling her fingers into the lushness of it the night before as he took her to the dizzying heights of absolute pleasure and far, far beyond. The connection she felt with him when his body joined with hers indescribable and totally scary. It was everything she had unknowingly craved and more.

Her heart sped up inside her chest.

He was so powerfully male, standing there with his arms on the balustrade, his muscular legs tanned and long beneath the white robe. He was a miracle of manhood in the prime of his life and he was all hers—or temporarily all hers. Temporarily and fakely all hers.

Fakely?

It wasn't even a word, but it described their situation perfectly. A situation that was fake but didn't quite feel fake. At least not for her.

Or at least not right now.

When she had agreed to this deal over a week ago she had imagined her biggest challenge would be to convince his family that they were a couple. In the end that had been the easy part. The hard part was keeping her hands off her boss-cum-fake-boyfriend and in that she had most definitely not succeeded.

But she wasn't going to dwell on that now. She knew what this was. She knew he was out of her league and that he had no long-term intentions towards her. Just as she had none towards him.

Sure, a cool voice in her head mocked, *if he wanted more, you'd jump at the chance.*

'Buongiorno.' His deep, sexy voice dragged her eyes up to his. 'How did you sleep?'

Knowing that she had been caught staring, she felt suddenly shy. 'Like a log.'

'Then I must not have been doing my job properly.' He held his hand out to her, beckoning her into his arms. 'It's a beautiful morning; come see.'

Pushing her wistful thoughts to the back of her mind, Poppy slipped into place, relaxing in his solid embrace, her back to his front. His arms tightened around her, his chin resting on the crown of her head. 'What did I tell you?'

Momentarily confused, Poppy realised he was talking about the view, and she forced herself to focus on the slumbering ancient city as the sun gilded the rooftops bronze and gold. 'It's exquisite. Maryann told me it was but I thought she was exaggerating.'

'Who is this Maryann to you?' he asked quietly.

'Maryann is a saviour to me. She lost her husband to cancer many years ago and when she found us we were like lost souls.' She smiled at the memory.

'Found *us*?'

'Simon and I.'

Sebastiano frowned. 'How old were you?'

Not wanting to ruin the moment by delving into the past, Poppy spoke quickly. 'I was seventeen. Simon was seven. Is that the island of Murano over there? I hear they have fantastic glassware for sale.'

Turning her in the circle of his arms, Sebastiano studied her face. 'Explain.'

Knowing she was thwarted, she pulled a face and let her mind drift back to that awful time, hoping he wouldn't look at her differently at the end of it. 'The day I met Maryann, I was at Paddington station trying to find a warm place for Simon to sleep since he was sick and—'

'Trying to find a warm place to sleep?' His voice deepened in alarm. 'Why didn't you go home? Or to a hospital, if your brother was ill?'

'I couldn't go to a hospital because I wasn't yet eighteen and I was afraid Social Services would separate us.' She bit her lip. 'And we didn't have a home.'

'Why not?'

She swallowed heavily. 'The last foster home we were placed in wasn't great and—I thought I could do better on my own.' She gave a self-mocking little laugh. 'Turns out I was pretty naïve on that score.'

'Go on.'

'Do I have to?'

He gave her a look that she knew from working for him scared CEOs and chairmen everywhere.

'Fine.' She rolled her eyes. 'I met a guy on the train to London and I was taken in by him. He was well-spoken and well-dressed and I somehow confided my situation to him. Looking back, I think I wanted to believe that there were good people in the world, so when he offered to help us out by lending us his spare room I jumped at the chance.'

A muscle ticked in Sebastiano's jaw. 'I'm not going to like where this story is headed, am I?'

Poppy pulled a face. 'Suffice to say he wanted payment

for the room, but not of a fiscal variety, and I told him I wasn't interested.'

'What did the lowlife do then?' His voice was so deep, Poppy blinked in surprise.

'He forced me to wake Simon and threw us out onto the street.' She didn't tell him she had been so foolish she had taken all her money out of her bank account so that Social Services couldn't trace her and he'd stolen the lot. That was too excruciatingly shameful.

Sebastiano swore viciously under his breath. '*Maledizione*, Poppy, you could have been hurt. Or killed.'

'It's just lucky Simon is deaf because he slept through the whole thing.'

'Your brother is deaf?' His eyebrows hit his hairline.

'Yes, but it doesn't define who he is. He's a perfectly normal teenage boy.'

'And you've taken care of him your whole life?'

'Since he was two. I used to throw a hissy fit whenever the social workers tried to separate us. It nearly didn't work on one occasion, but basically no one wanted a deaf toddler, and he would only be soothed when I was around.'

Sebastiano stared down at her, some of the steely rage that had come into his eyes easing. 'You're amazing, you know that?' He cupped her face in his hands. 'Strong. Sexy. Beautiful. Inside and out.'

'Don't,' she said, uncomfortable hearing his praise. She was nothing special and it was only a matter of time before he figured that out.

'You are,' he asserted softly. 'But I agree.' He sat down in the corner chair and tugged on the belt of her robe. 'We have done enough talking.' He kissed a trail down her midline and turned her to face the railing.

'What are you doing?' she asked breathlessly.

'I'm going to show you how you make me feel. Bend

forward, *bella*,' he crooned in her ear, placing her hands on the balustrading. 'And don't let go.'

Hours later Sebastiano jolted awake; the only sound in the room was Poppy's soft breathing as she lay beside him. Carefully, he turned his head to confirm that she was sleeping. She was, her soft curves pressed into his side, her kiss-swollen lips parted, her silky hair spread out on the pillow.

Their love-making this time had been different from the other times. Less intense, but somehow more powerful. If that was even possible.

He adjusted the bedcovers over her shoulder and she nestled deeper against him. He smiled and slid his hand over her thigh. Her skin felt like silk beneath his rougher fingertips. She sighed, a whisper of a sound that feathered across his chest. He contemplated waking her up, kissing her brow, her cheeks, the little dimple beside her mouth. She was so responsive to his touch he could already imagine her turning towards him, arching against him, giving him one of those tiny whimpers he loved so much.

Dio, this was supposed to have been just one more night. Not that either of them had stipulated as much—but, regardless, he had thought that was all it would be and now, if he was honest, he wanted more. The irony of which was not lost on him.

And somewhere in his psyche he must have known this would happen because on the flight to Venice he had decided to put as much distance between them as possible.

Si, Castiglione, you tried really hard.

Annoyed with himself, he gently extracted his arm from beneath Poppy's neck and headed for the shower.

Damn it, he *had* tried. Only she had worn him down.

By breathing?

He hit the shower mixer and hot water jetted out over his tense body.

The thing was that opening up about his parents the previous night had made him feel vulnerable. Somehow she milked information out of him like a zookeeper getting venom from a snake. If he wasn't careful he'd be depleted before he knew it.

And what about her story on the terrace? *Por Dio*, he was still reeling from that, and he wanted to hunt down the animal who had jumped her and beat him to a pulp. Her experiences in life were far worse than anything he had been forced to face yet she didn't seem to feel sorry for herself the way he sometimes did.

He shoved his head under a water jet.

What had started out one-hundred-percent fake had at some point during the weekend shifted to being only fifty-percent fake. And that fifty percent was all on her side. Because once he'd taken her into his bed it had become real for him, and now he didn't want it to end.

Not yet anyway.

And why should it? They weren't hurting anyone. They weren't breaking any laws. What they were doing was working this attraction out of their systems until it was no longer there.

A slow, satisfied smile broke across his face and he felt lighter as he towelled himself off. More in control. He padded out into the bedroom. Working this attraction out of their systems made complete sense.

'Rise and shine, sleepy head. The Guggenheim awaits.'

Poppy groaned and covered her head with a pillow. 'If you've seen one painting, you've seen them all.'

Sebastiano grinned. 'Sacrilegious, intern! Picasso is rolling over in his grave about now.'

'Picasso could be skywriting outside our window and I wouldn't care,' she grumbled.

Laughing softly, he lifted the pillow from her head and bent to kiss her.

Had he ever felt this happy?

Yes, he thought as a feather-stroke of unease raised the hair along his forearms. His grin faded. He'd felt this happy when he'd been a child. Blindingly, blissfully happy, and completely unaware of how easily all that could be lost with one bad decision.

By the time Sebastiano's jet touched down in Naples it was late and Poppy's joy at the day had morphed into something mellower. Giuseppe's smiling limo driver greeted them and put his foot down as he whisked them through the dusky evening towards Villa Castiglione.

A soft, dreamy smile curved her lips as her mind drifted over the afternoon they had shared in Venice: eating pizza beneath a shop awning to dodge the rain, checking out the Guggenheim and visiting the island of Murano where she had bought two small glass figurines, one for her brother and one for Maryann. Sebastiano had also bought her a tiny bluebird he'd said was the exact colour of her eyes when she was happy.

It had all been so perfect. So wonderfully normal she had quite forgotten that it wasn't. Had Sebastiano forgotten too? Did he feel any of the things she did?

She glanced at his carved profile. Being with him was like a dream, a dream she never wanted to wake up from. But the closer they got to the Villa, the closer they got to flying home to London, and the real world. The real world where yet again she would be required to be stoic and move on when things didn't work out as she hoped.

Memories of past homes she and Simon had stayed at crowded in on her. Not all of them had been bad. Some had seemed almost promising but in the end even those families hadn't wanted them. Not long term.

Feeling her stomach pitch Poppy pressed her hand to her abdomen. Sebastiano noticed.

'Everything okay?'

'Of course,' she murmured, staring at their hands as he linked their fingers together.

The fact was she would follow Sebastiano's lead on this. She would collect the things they had left at the villa the day before, say goodbye when he dropped her at her front door, maybe shake his hand, thank him for everything and— Oh God, the third wish...

She had nearly forgotten about the third wish.

Her throat tightened. She had already decided to let that go. How could she not when she loved him so much? Because, yes, she did love him, she acknowledged with a sigh. What was the point in denying it to herself any longer?

But she had a sneaking suspicion that Sebastiano wouldn't let her off the hook about that last wish so easily. He wasn't a man who left his debts unpaid, another thing that made him so lovable.

But what could she ask for when he was the only thing she wanted? The one thing she couldn't have because, even though he had said he wanted her, even though they had shared another night together, nothing had really changed between them. She was still Poppy Connolly, the daughter of a drug user, and he was still Sebastiano Castiglione, descendent of a royal household. Their getting together would be like Zeus pairing up with a Hyde Park squirrel!

'Look at the colour of the sea,' she said, wanting to distract herself. 'It's almost black in this light.'

'Yes.'

'And those houses.' She crinkled her nose. 'Maintenance must be really difficult, seeing as how they're built so close together. Do you think—? Hey!'

Suddenly she felt his hands on her waist. 'I want to see you in London.'

His roughly spoken words startled her and she must

have stared at him a full minute before responding, elation sending a wave of emotion through her whole body. 'Did I just hear you right?'

'*Si*. Our relationship might have started out fake, but it's not fake any more.' He flashed her a quick smile, his eyes searing her with a blaze of heat. 'Why end things prematurely when we don't have to?'

Reeling from his request, and his warm hands either side of her waist, a laugh welled up inside her. What had started out as fake for her had turned real in a very short space of time too.

Very real.

But continue to see him in London? A niggle in the back of her mind stopped her from jumping at the idea and throwing her hands around his neck. A niggle that warned her that if something was too good to be true then it usually was.

'But how do we make it work?' she asked, easing back from him. 'I have so little free time as it is. And…' She shrugged helplessly. 'Between our two schedules we'd never get to see each other.'

'I'll make it work.'

Poppy rolled her eyes at his confident tone. 'But how? Give me the logistics.'

'The logistics, Miss Connolly?' He smiled and kissed her. 'The logistics are that I'm going to get you a new place. Somewhere I'm a little less likely to lose a wheel whenever I visit.'

'A new place?'

'And you can quit your night job. I'll give you an allowance I think you'll find more than generous.'

'An allowance?'

He smiled indulgently. 'That's right. Your new role is to be exclusively mine.'

A lump formed in Poppy's throat. 'You're doing that

earth-moving thing again,' she said thickly, unable to take in everything he was saying.

'Not yet I'm not.' He nuzzled kisses along her neck. 'But give me time.'

She laughed. 'Sebastiano, be serious.'

'I've never been more serious.' His smile was panther-like. 'Say yes.'

The car pulled up smoothly outside the villa and Poppy stared at it absently. Her mind was foggy and, even though she knew she shouldn't, she said the only thing in her head to say. 'Yes, but—'

Before she could voice her objections about the apartment and the allowance Sebastiano kissed her soundly, rendering the thinking part of her brain obsolete.

Sebastiano poured more wine in Poppy's glass as she recounted their trip to Venice, to the delight of his transfixed grandparents. They couldn't get enough of Poppy. It was as if she had cast a spell over all of them. Even Lukas had been taken by her, and Eleanore had texted him earlier in the day asking for Poppy's number so they could catch up when she was next in London.

If he wasn't careful, Sebastiano thought bemusedly, she would become a permanent fixture in his life without him even noticing it.

A cool sense of disquiet brushed over his skin like a spider's web and he swept it aside.

Poppy already knew that he didn't do permanent and, after all, it wasn't his apartment he intended to set her up in.

He grinned as he recalled her shocked face when he had suggested it. All those claims about him not being her type—in the end she had jumped at the chance to sleep with him, as he had her, and she certainly hadn't put the brakes on things since then, despite her claim that sleeping with him had been a mistake. That had surprised him a little, but hell, who was he to complain?

He slowly twirled the wine in his glass and glanced across at her. She'd worn another one of the outfits he'd provided for her and he loved seeing her wearing his clothes. He loved seeing her smiling as she was now, her eyes sparkly like the bluebird he hadn't been able to resist getting her on Murano.

His grandmother was talking and he tuned back in before his *nonno* accused him of daydreaming.

'That would be lovely,' Poppy murmured carefully.

Sebastiano frowned, catching her guilty look. He raised an eyebrow. *What would be lovely?*

She dabbed her mouth with her napkin. 'I know Simon would love to meet you both too. And Maryann. And I can cook lunch if you like?'

She was going to cook lunch for his grandparents?

Sebastiano's eyebrow rose higher. What on earth was she talking about?

This wasn't supposed to be a long-term arrangement; he hoped she realised that. He was happy to set her up in an apartment, visit her whenever he wanted, but as to the rest—as to her playing domestic goddess for his family... And what about her family? He hadn't even thought about meeting them.

And how exactly was he going to call in on her with her brother hanging around? How would that look to a young teenager? 'Yes, hello, I've just come over to make love to your sister.'

If some guy had tried that with Nicolette, he'd have floored him.

Sweat broke out on his forehead, a sick feeling clawing at his stomach. And why *had* Poppy jumped at the chance to move into an apartment?

Little Miss I Like Paying My Own Bills hadn't so much

as batted an eyelash when he'd told her. It was almost as if she had been waiting for him to offer it.

He frowned. Had he been taken in by a slick operator? Had he, a man who'd had women try every trick in the book to turn his head, fallen for the oldest one of all? The one who played hard to get?

'Sebastiano, you've gone pale,' his grandmother said.

Sebastiano carefully put down his knife and fork. *'Si; scusa, Nonna.'* He pushed back from the table. 'Poppy and I have to leave.'

'Is something wrong?'

Poppy nearly rolled her eyes at her own stupid question. Was the sky blue? Was the Arctic cold? Yes, but not as cold as Sebastiano's expression as he stood before her with his hands on his hips.

'Why did my grandparents say they were coming to London?'

'I'm not sure.'

He folded his arms across his chest. 'Why did you offer to cook them lunch?'

'I didn't mean to do that.' She laughed nervously, not understanding where this was headed. 'I'm a terrible cook but when they said they were coming to visit it just popped out.'

His dark brows climbed his forehead. 'It just popped out?'

'Yes. Why are you looking at me like that?' She frowned. 'What would you have had me say? That I wouldn't have them over?'

'No, of course not.' He ran a hand through his hair. 'I just—I just wasn't expecting it.'

Poppy gnawed on the inside of her cheek. Why wasn't he taking her in his arms? Why wasn't he kissing her? 'And?'

He paced away from her and stared out of the window. 'And what?'

'And what else is wrong?' Suddenly her heart felt heavy instead of light. 'Are you regretting telling me that you want to continue our relationship? Is that why you've gone all broody?'

'I haven't gone all broody.'

'Yes you have. And you were very quiet at dinner and now you can barely look at me.'

'You're exaggerating,' he said with a small laugh. 'And what happened to "Bastian"?'

'Excuse me?'

'You called me Bastian in Venice.'

Well, she'd felt closer to him in Venice. The man in front of her now was the one who had greeted her yesterday morning after regretting the night before. The polite stranger. Poppy felt her stomach roil again. 'Did I?'

'Yes, you did. You were also very quick to jump at my offer to set you up in an apartment. Is that the place you were imagining cooking for my grandparents?'

'Yes,' she said evenly, suddenly understanding what was motivating Sebastiano's strange behaviour. 'I pictured a lovely galley kitchen with slate tiles and, eh, oak cabinets.' Poppy wracked her brain for what else an expensive kitchen would have as hurt and outrage roiled inside her stomach. She had thought—she had imagined—that he had fallen for her too. 'And a stainless steel splashback,' she finished with a belligerent flourish.

'Really?'

Sebastiano had come to a stop in front of her and Poppy wanted to hit him for not being able to see that she was hurting. That she wasn't the kind of person he was silently accusing her of being. Hit him and rail at him for hurting her so much. For making her believe in fairy tales again. 'Yes.' She tilted her chin up, unable to stop herself. 'And then I thought we'd retire to the living area and have wine on the marble terrace overlooking St Paul's Cathedral. You are intending to get me an apartment overlooking St Paul's Cathedral, aren't you?'

'Poppy?'

'Yes, *Bastian*?'

'I'm sorry.' He crossed the room and put his arms around her. 'I shouldn't have said what I did.'

Poppy carefully stepped out of his embrace. 'No, you shouldn't have.'

He frowned as she moved toward the bedroom. 'Where are you going?'

'To pack,' she said wearily. Anywhere really where he wouldn't see the tears glittering behind her eyes.

'You're angry.'

'Yes. But it's with myself, so don't worry about it. I'm the one who should have known better.'

'Poppy, listen.' He grabbed her again and swung her around to face him. 'You can hardly blame me for thinking what I just did. You said yourself that this is like a fairy tale. You wanted me to pinch you, remember?'

'I remember.' She gave him a smile but everything inside her had already closed down and moved on. Now all she had to do was fetch her bags. 'Excuse me.'

'Don't be unreasonable about this.'

Poppy threw her own clothes into her duffle bag, hurt now morphing into anger. *Don't be unreasonable?*

'I mean, you were the one who came into my office that Sunday morning in your sexy jeans and tight sweater and telling my grandfather you could handle me. Can you really blame me if I briefly wondered if you had been hoping something like this would happen?'

'Not at all,' she said blithely. 'In fact, you're right. I was hoping your grandfather would walk in and think we were a couple so we could pretend to be one, and eventually you would fall in love with me so we could live happily ever after in a penthouse in the sky. A great plan don't you think?'

A muscle ticked in his jaw. 'I'm sorry. I was wrong to say what I did.'

'Yes you were.' She stood before him, her duffle bag in her hand. 'But you thought it and the truth is…' Poppy swallowed heavily. 'The truth is you don't want more from me than a temporary affair anyway. So in the end it's irrelevant.'

He raked a hand through his hair. 'Are you saying you do?'

'No.' She stared at him. His words, his very aloofness, confirmed everything she already knew. He didn't want her. Not really. Not in the way she wanted him. 'But I will ask for my third wish.'

His gaze turned wary. 'What is it?'

'That we never see each other again.'

CHAPTER FOURTEEN

'YOU ARE HEADING back to London, I see?'

Sebastiano didn't look up as his grandfather entered the library, just continued to stare at the photo in his hand before he set it aside. 'Yes. It was a good idea to spend the week in the Rome office. I feel as if I've got a handle on everything that needs to be done now.' He set his laptop in his carry-on bag. He'd do more work on the plane, though God knew he was so tired he might just crash instead. And wouldn't that be a godsend? The blissful oblivion of sleep.

'And will you be seeing Poppy in London?'

'No.' He knew his grandfather had sensed something wrong between them when she had bid them a teary good-bye last Monday night, but they'd respected his unwillingness to talk about it, as they had done in the past.

'Why not?'

The frown on his grandfather's face told a thousand stories. The most blatant being that Sebastiano had disappointed him. Again.

'Because Poppy was never a long-term proposition,' he grated, knowing it was the truth. He was a loner. It was how he had conditioned himself since his parents' deaths. Poppy leaving when she did had been a good thing. Hurting her hadn't but—he didn't want to think about how that made him feel.

'Proposition?' His grandfather frowned. 'What kind of a word is this to use about a woman like Poppy?'

Sebastiano swore under his breath. 'Look I have an admission to make.' He held his grandfather's gaze. 'It doesn't make me feel particularly proud of myself, but it's done and I can't change it.' He grimaced. 'I lied to you about my relationship with Poppy to force you to retire and hand me CE. So, if you want to reverse your decision and pass the job onto someone else—the CFO?—I won't argue.'

'Stefan is not the right man for the job. And he is not family.'

'You're going to have to move with the times at some point, Nonno.' He ran a hand through his hair, his chest tight. 'I'll support whatever decision you want to make.'

'You are the only man for the job. You always were.'

Sebastiano grimaced. 'You mean my father was.'

'*Si*. But he is not here. And it is time you stopped living in the past which you cannot change.'

'I do not live in the past.'

'You do. But what is this lie you speak of? I did not see a lie between you and Poppy.'

'You thought we were a couple.' And they had been for a short while. 'We weren't.'

His grandfather frowned. 'When did I say you were a couple?'

'In my office. You said…' His eyes narrowed. What exactly had his grandfather said? 'You told me to bring her here for the party. To meet Nonna.'

'*Si*. Why would I not? She is a beautiful young woman. I saw something between you and I thought she was the one to bring you alive again. And I was right. She did. Now your stubborn pride is going to ruin everything.'

Sebastiano stared at the man who had taken over the job of raising him after his parents had died. Then he shook his head.

'*Dio*, you're right.'

'I usually am.' His grandfather laid his hand on his shoulder. 'How long are you going to keep punishing yourself for what happened fifteen years ago, *nipote mio*?' he asked quietly.

For ever.

The words jumped into his head, startling him. Was he really going to blame himself for ever?

And how could he have treated Poppy the way that he had? How could he have thought she was after him for his money? His status? She, the woman who had baulked at him buying her a small figurine, and who had refused to let him have the Guggenheim opened because she hadn't wanted to wake the curator. *Cristo.* Any other woman he had dated would have simpered about how important he was.

He stared down at the photo he'd unconsciously picked up again. He swallowed heavily. 'Here,' he said gruffly, handing to his grandfather the photo he'd found facedown in a drawer. 'This belongs on Nonna's photo wall, doesn't it?'

'Si,' his grandfather said thickly, his gaze riveted to the photo of Sebastiano and his parents taken the day before their fatal accident.

They looked at each other a long time, understanding flowing between them. The abominable weight Sebastiano had carried around for too long slowly easing.

'What about Poppy?' his grandfather prompted.

Sebastiano took a deep breath. With the clarity of how much he had held himself back came the realisation that it had been easier to let Poppy walk away than to face his own feelings. 'I stuffed up.'

Because without a doubt in his mind he loved her. Completely and totally.

'I told your grandmother that this time I was not going to respect your privacy and let you try and work this out for yourself. You are too thick headed.'

Sebastiano shook his head. 'I should be angry with you.'

'*Si.*' His grandfather waved him off, his eyes suspiciously moist. 'You can thank me later.'

'It sounds like a Cinderella story!' Maryann sighed.

Yes, it did, Poppy thought. Even up to her leaving the silvery gown and shoes behind as if they'd never existed. 'It's not a Cinderella story. Cinderella wasn't studying law, and she had magic mice to help her along.' And the Prince had searched the land for Cinderella afterwards, but already a week had gone by and she'd not heard a word from Sebastiano. She didn't even know what country he was in. 'And there are more important things to worry about. Like you. How are you? What did the doctor say today?'

'I'm fine. My tingling wasn't so bad yesterday and my hands aren't numb at all today. And I start the new drug trials next week, which should reverse that even more.'

'That's great.'

Every day since she had walked out on Sebastiano Poppy had expected someone to come knocking on her door and take back the trainers and the keys to Maryann's apartment. So far they hadn't. But deep down she knew they wouldn't. It was what she had asked for after all and Sebastiano was definitely a man of his word.

Poppy glanced around at the large bay windows that looked out over a small front garden and the wonderful green parkland opposite. Maryann's apartment was beyond the scope of Poppy's expectations and she didn't know how Sebastiano had managed to organise such a perfect place so quickly, but then maybe she did. When he wanted something, there wasn't much that stood in his way.

But she wasn't supposed to be thinking about him any more.

She glanced over at where Simon was absorbed in a video game. 'Are you sure you're okay having Simon stay over tonight?' She'd taken a double shift to make up for

Monday night and she didn't like Simon being alone for so long.

'Of course. He's an enormous help to me, Poppy.'

Poppy smiled at her beautiful brother. 'He's the best,' she agreed.

She heaved a heavy sigh. 'How do you do it?' she asked Maryann. 'How do you forge on when it all seems so hopeless?'

'I try and remember that there's always something to be grateful for, no matter how small.'

'God, you're wise,' Poppy choked out. 'I'm so lucky to have found you.'

She wrapped her arms around the woman who had literally saved her life.

'I think I'm the lucky one, Poppy. You brightened my life the day you came into it.'

Poppy scrubbed at her eyes. 'I was a mess.'

'You were.'

They laughed and held each other.

Later, on the Tube, Poppy looked around at the various commuters, most with their heads bent over their mobile phones. As heavy as she felt right now, she did have a lot to be grateful for. Simon. Maryann. The lovely cleaning crew she would be working with tonight. The fact that she would always have the memory of Italy and how she had once spilled coffee over one of the most powerful businessmen on the globe. How she had once slept in his arms for one glorious weekend. How she had loved him. How she would always love him…

Her breath caught and she stumbled to her feet as her train pulled into her stop. She kept her head down as she followed the mass of commuters to the nearest exit and didn't even feel the rain as it fell over her bent head.

Dodging the late-night traffic, she headed into the first

building they would be cleaning tonight, a large one off Charing Cross.

She had found comfort in working this week, getting herself into a rhythm that exhausted her to the point she couldn't think too much.

Two hours in, she dropped her rag into a bucket and stretched her back.

'Hey, popsicle. Want a coffee? Bernie's heading out to the shop across the street.'

Convenience store coffee? *Brilliant!* 'Love one,' she said. 'Thanks, Tom.' She had been spoiled by authentic Italian coffee but she was going to have to get over that. The quicker, the better.

Finishing up another office, Poppy was just doing an inventory to make sure she hadn't missed anything when she heard Bernie return. 'Just put it on the desk, Bernie. Thanks.'

'It's not Bernie.'

Startled by the sound of Sebastiano's deep voice, Poppy swung around, the long feather duster tucked under her arm sweeping out and catching him on the elbow. He made to dodge it, the to-go cup of coffee he was holding flying upwards, a spray of milky liquid fountaining out and landing all over his clean shirt.

A string of Italian curse words left his mouth. 'Are you kidding me?'

Poppy stared at him open-mouthed. 'Oh God, I'm so sorry.' Then her brain came online. 'Sebastiano! What are you doing here?'

'Looking for you.' He shook his head and pulled at his shirt. 'And getting covered in coffee. Again.'

Galvanised by his words Poppy grabbed a wad of tissues and thrust them at him. He took them and stared at her.

Please don't look at me like that, she thought, wrapping her arms around her waist. 'Why are you looking for me?'

He sat the half-empty cup on the desk and took a deep breath. 'I was looking for you because about five hours ago I realised I've been a monumental idiot and I wanted to tell you that I love you and ask you to marry me. I thought it would be better to do it face-to-face than over the phone.'

Poppy's jaw hit the floor. 'I'm sorry?'

'So am I, *bella*. I'm sorry I panicked and made you feel less than you are the other night. I'm sorry it's taken me a week to figure everything out and I'm sorry I associated love with pain for so long I actually believed I was better off without it.' He swallowed heavily. 'But I'm not. Better off, that is. You've shown me that.'

'I have?'

'Absolutely. You face everything that happens to you head-on and you only look for the best in others. I on the other hand look for the worst. Looked.' He smiled faintly. 'Past tense. But I love you, Poppy, with all my heart, and I know I promised to give you three wishes but that last one... If you want me to honour it of course I will, but you have to know it's not what I want.'

Poppy's heart climbed into her throat. She wanted so much to believe him but she knew she was difficult to love. Difficult to have around. 'Sebastiano—'

Sebastiano stepped closer, clasping her shaking hands in his. 'I know you're scared, *amore mia*. I am too, but I'm taking a leaf out of your book and going with what feels right.'

Poppy felt light-headed. 'You are?'

'I am.' He smiled softly. 'I've been walking around half-alive before you came into my life and I don't want to live like that anymore.'

He drew her forward slowly and Poppy went, still wondering if she wouldn't wake up and find this was all a lovely dream. 'I think I might need you to pinch me.'

'To prove this isn't real?'

'To prove that it is.' She gave him a tremulous smile. 'I can't believe this is happening.'

'That's because you've been let down by too many of the people closest to you,' he said gently. 'Including me.' He put his arms around her waist. 'I knew something was up when my grandfather handed me the CEO position and it didn't make me happy. That was one of the reasons I was drinking. Apart from it being the night my parents died, I couldn't face what it said about me. Not until you pushed me to feel again. I love you, Poppy, and if you'll let me I'll gladly spend the rest of my life proving it to you.'

Tears shone in Poppy's eyes.

Sebastiano went down on bended knee, pulling a ring box out of his pocket. 'Traditionally giving you things hasn't gone well for me. I'm hoping this time will be the exception.'

He opened the box and an enormous diamond winked back, dazzling her. 'Oh, my God. I will get mugged wearing that!'

'No, you won't, because I'll be there to protect you.' He took her hand in his. 'Poppy Connolly, will you marry me and let me love you and take care of you and Simon and Maryann for the rest of my life?'

'Blimey, Poppy, if you don't say yes, I will.'

Bernie's impromptu interruption from the doorway made Poppy laugh. She swiped at the tears leaking out of the corner of her eyes.

'Sorry, love, I didn't mean to interrupt,' Bernie said sheepishly. 'I was just checking on you. I'll tell Tom you're otherwise disposed.'

Poppy stared at Sebastiano, so happy she thought she might burst. 'I didn't exactly fight for what I felt the other night either. I think deep down I expected you to ditch me, and so when it seemed like you were I went into survival mode.'

'I don't blame you. Can you forgive me?'

'Of course I can forgive you,' she said softly. 'I love you.'

Sebastiano groaned and rose to his feet, pulling her into his arms and kissing her. 'Is that a yes to my proposal, then?'

She smiled up at him. 'Are you going to offer me another three wishes if I say no?'

A grin spread slowly across his face. 'No, you're going to give me three wishes this time.'

'Oh?'

'Yes. Wish number one is that you don't ever bring me coffee again.' He grimaced as he glanced at his chest and Poppy realised they were both now covered in coffee! 'You were actually bringing me coffee this time,' she pointed out, almost giddy with the happiness fit to burst from inside her chest.

'Two: you walk around naked in our house for the rest of your life.'

'That is so not going to happen.' She laughed. 'And three?'

'Three: you promise to love me for ever, even though I'm likely to stuff up from time to time.'

'Deal,' she said, wrapping her arms around his neck. 'Oh God, Bastian. I love you so much.'

'Grazie a Dio,' he said softly. 'Now, you need to text Simon and Maryann. They said if they hadn't heard from you within the hour they were sending out a search party. Maryann also said to say thank you for her new apartment.'

'You told her?'

'I didn't have to. You have a terrible poker face, *amore mia.*' He scooped her into his arms.

'I know. I really need to change that.'

'Don't change it. I don't want you to change a hair on your beautiful head. You're perfect, Poppy. My perfect Poppy.'

She clung to him, her arms tight around his neck. 'I feel like I'm in a scene from a movie.'

'You're not. This is one-hundred-percent real. And every year we're going to celebrate in Venice. Would you like that?'

'I don't care where I am as long as you're by my side.'

'For ever, intern. For ever.'

* * * * *

If you enjoyed
THE ITALIAN'S VIRGIN ACQUISITION
why not explore these other
Michelle Conder stories?

DEFYING THE BILLIONAIRE'S COMMAND
HIDDEN IN THE SHEIKH'S HAREM
RUSSIAN'S RUTHLESS DEMAND
PRINCE NADIR'S SECRET HEIR
SOCIALITE'S GAMBLE

Available now!

MILLS & BOON®
Hardback – September 2017

ROMANCE

The Tycoon's Outrageous Proposal	Miranda Lee
Cipriani's Innocent Captive	Cathy Williams
Claiming His One-Night Baby	Michelle Smart
At the Ruthless Billionaire's Command	Carole Mortimer
Engaged for Her Enemy's Heir	Kate Hewitt
His Drakon Runaway Bride	Tara Pammi
The Throne He Must Take	Chantelle Shaw
The Italian's Virgin Acquisition	Michelle Conder
A Proposal from the Crown Prince	Jessica Gilmore
Sarah and the Secret Sheikh	Michelle Douglas
Conveniently Engaged to the Boss	Ellie Darkins
Her New York Billionaire	Andrea Bolter
The Doctor's Forbidden Temptation	Tina Beckett
From Passion to Pregnancy	Tina Beckett
The Midwife's Longed-For Baby	Caroline Anderson
One Night That Changed Her Life	Emily Forbes
The Prince's Cinderella Bride	Amalie Berlin
Bride for the Single Dad	Jennifer Taylor
A Family for the Billionaire	Dani Wade
Taking Home the Tycoon	Catherine Mann

MILLS & BOON®
Large Print – September 2017

ROMANCE

The Sheikh's Bought Wife	Sharon Kendrick
The Innocent's Shameful Secret	Sara Craven
The Magnate's Tempestuous Marriage	Miranda Lee
The Forced Bride of Alazar	Kate Hewitt
Bound by the Sultan's Baby	Carol Marinelli
Blackmailed Down the Aisle	Louise Fuller
Di Marcello's Secret Son	Rachael Thomas
Conveniently Wed to the Greek	Kandy Shepherd
His Shy Cinderella	Kate Hardy
Falling for the Rebel Princess	Ellie Darkins
Claimed by the Wealthy Magnate	Nina Milne

HISTORICAL

The Secret Marriage Pact	Georgie Lee
A Warriner to Protect Her	Virginia Heath
Claiming His Defiant Miss	Bronwyn Scott
Rumours at Court (Rumors at Court)	Blythe Gifford
The Duke's Unexpected Bride	Lara Temple

MEDICAL

Their Secret Royal Baby	Carol Marinelli
Her Hot Highland Doc	Annie O'Neil
His Pregnant Royal Bride	Amy Ruttan
Baby Surprise for the Doctor Prince	Robin Gianna
Resisting Her Army Doc Rival	Sue MacKay
A Month to Marry the Midwife	Fiona McArthur

MILLS & BOON®
Hardback – October 2017

ROMANCE

Claimed for the Leonelli Legacy	Lynne Graham
The Italian's Pregnant Prisoner	Maisey Yates
Buying His Bride of Convenience	Michelle Smart
The Tycoon's Marriage Deal	Melanie Milburne
Undone by the Billionaire Duke	Caitlin Crews
His Majesty's Temporary Bride	Annie West
Bound by the Millionaire's Ring	Dani Collins
The Virgin's Shock Baby	Heidi Rice
Whisked Away by Her Sicilian Boss	Rebecca Winters
The Sheikh's Pregnant Bride	Jessica Gilmore
A Proposal from the Italian Count	Lucy Gordon
Claiming His Secret Royal Heir	Nina Milne
Sleigh Ride with the Single Dad	Alison Roberts
A Firefighter in Her Stocking	Janice Lynn
A Christmas Miracle	Amy Andrews
Reunited with Her Surgeon Prince	Marion Lennox
Falling for Her Fake Fiancé	Sue MacKay
The Family She's Longed For	Lucy Clark
Billionaire Boss, Holiday Baby	Janice Maynard
Billionaire's Baby Bind	Katherine Garbera

MILLS & BOON®
Large Print – October 2017

ROMANCE

Sold for the Greek's Heir	Lynne Graham
The Prince's Captive Virgin	Maisey Yates
The Secret Sanchez Heir	Cathy Williams
The Prince's Nine-Month Scandal	Caitlin Crews
Her Sinful Secret	Jane Porter
The Drakon Baby Bargain	Tara Pammi
Xenakis's Convenient Bride	Dani Collins
Her Pregnancy Bombshell	Liz Fielding
Married for His Secret Heir	Jennifer Faye
Behind the Billionaire's Guarded Heart	Leah Ashton
A Marriage Worth Saving	Therese Beharrie

HISTORICAL

The Debutante's Daring Proposal	Annie Burrows
The Convenient Felstone Marriage	Jenni Fletcher
An Unexpected Countess	Laurie Benson
Claiming His Highland Bride	Terri Brisbin
Marrying the Rebellious Miss	Bronwyn Scott

MEDICAL

Their One Night Baby	Carol Marinelli
Forbidden to the Playboy Surgeon	Fiona Lowe
A Mother to Make a Family	Emily Forbes
The Nurse's Baby Secret	Janice Lynn
The Boss Who Stole Her Heart	Jennifer Taylor
Reunited by Their Pregnancy Surprise	Louisa Heaton